D0779856

Welcome to the OASIS

AND
OTHER
STORIES

Virgil Suárez

Arte Publico Press
Houston
Texas
1992

This book is made possible through a grant from the National Endowment for the Arts, a federal agency.

Arte Publico Press
University of Houston
Houston, Texas 77204-2090

Cover design by Mark Piñón

Suárez, Virgil, 1962–
    Welcome to the Oasis & other stories / by Virgil Suárez.
        p.   cm.
    Contents: Welcome to the Oasis — Dearly beloved — A perfect hotspot — Full house — Settlements — Headshots.
    ISBN 1-55885-043-0
    1. Hispanic Americans—Fiction. I. Title. II. Title: Welcome to the Oasis and other stories.
PS3569.U18W4 1992
813'.54–dc20   91-31374

                                                                                    CIP

The paper used in this publication meets the requirements of the American National Standard for Permanence of Paper for Printed Library Materials Z39.48-1984. ∞

Copyright © 1992 by Virgil Suárez
Printed in the United States of America

For Vance Bourjaily, friend and mentor

Sucede que me canso de ser hombre.
　　　　　　　　　　　—Pablo Neruda

Welcome to the Oasis
and Other Stories

Welcome to the Oasis

I

BEYOND the train tracks on the other side of the city of Encantado, the apartments are hidden from the main street's traffic, but are not entirely immune from the brown haze of exhaust. The two buildings, divided by a diamond-shaped pool, stand cornered in their own lot of dry earth. They seem like relics, undisturbed, yet-to-be-found temples.

Uneven rows of pine and eucalyptus, whose needles and thin leaves fall and are swept up into circles on the scarred cement walkways by gusts of wind, and a trash-cluttered vacant lot surround the buildings. Behind a rusty, wrought iron fence, green moss covers the fountain that birds once bathed in under the nymph statuette. Tufts of weeds grow against the cracked stucco walls. Copper-green stains left by leaks from the rusted drainpipes ooze under the eaves.

Marks remain where the frame holding up the canvas awning at the entrance once belonged. There, underneath the arch, hangs a termite-ridden sign that reads OASIS APARTMENTS, with the T's erased.

II

IT happens while he scrapes the flaking paint off one of the upstairs windows. An apparition almost scares the painter off the thirty-foot ladder. A dark face wrapped in a red scarf draws near the smudged glass.

Feet on the last rung, he stands over the ash-colored ground which is speckled with millions of tiny paint flecks, his fingers letting go of the soft and furrowed wood of the windowsill.

The woman's eyes look like two marbles, two moons. Distant, yet alert, soft but riddled with unpleasant hardships. Greasy lips part and a set of teeth show. The glass panel slides open and the woman sticks her head out and says, "What are you doing?"

The painter hesitates, trying to find words.

"What devil sent you?" she says.

A man named Quiroga, he tells her, his boss and owner of the apartments.

"Quiroga, eh?"

She speaks in a slow, scratchy tone. Her appearance makes him think of a buzzard or a crow standing over carrion. She rests her large hands on the window frame. Her fingers look out of proportion, too long and black, wrinkled like claws. On her right wrist she wears a bundle of intertwined bracelets of different colored and odd-shaped beads, *caracoles* or cowries. Whenever she moves her hand, the bracelets make a sound similar to that of gold coins falling into a bag.

The smell of fried plantain and corn fritters escapes from the window.

"Are you—" she begins to say, but changes her mind, and says, "Where are you from?"

He tells her he came from Habana, Cuba.

"Arrived recently? Have you been here long?"

"At work, you mean?"

"Not at work, in California," she says.

"Yes, recently."

"How recent?"

"A year ago."

"That makes you a *Marielito*," she says, "you came from Mariel."

She leans back and stands silent for a brief moment, pensive, then she says, "Quiroga's not the man to work for."

"Work's work," he says.

"Treats *me* like shit."

"You manage this place?" he asks.

"Been doing so for ten years," she says. "Tell me, how did he find you?"

"I found him. I answered an ad in the paper."

The ad called for a reliable, hard-working, experienced painter.

"You shouldn't have, son. Just shouldn't." She stops to think, her eyes narrow under heavy black lids. "Quiroga's been here in the United States too long. I think it has affected him. Bah! He was probably the same way in the old country. People like him don't change. Not at all. All business and no heart. Greedy bastard."

Listening intently because he likes her interesting *santera* appearance, the painter leans forward on the ladder so that it doesn't sway.

She continues: "Been here too long, and he's been spoiled by wealth. He's made it, you see. And once you make it here, you think you are ... " She pauses to pull up a folding metal chair, sits down and lights a cigar stub she produces from her skirt pocket, a wrinkled cotton skirt worn so thin her dark legs show through.

Aside from her discontented look and haggard aspect, remnants of the beauty she once possessed, long ago, are still evident. She has a fine nose, full lips, high cheek bones and a friendly, compassionate smile.

The smoke floats around her face and head, becoming a veil, a turban.

"Look at me with that smile on your lips," she says, "but this *mulata* knows what she's talking about. Whatever you're doing here, do it quickly and go."

He is not sure what she is trying to tell him.

"Just started on the priming," he says. "Window work."

"Go!" she says, blowing a plume of smoke his way. "Yes, yes, finish as soon as you can and get away from here. Tell Quiroga to let you work on another of his properties. Got lots and lots. The last thing you want to do's work here."

"Might be finishing in three to four weeks, paint and all. Depends."

"Paint? He asked you to paint, eh? He's crazy. How dare he send— "

"Look, I can manage," the painter says. He grips the wire scrape brush tight in his hand.

"Stay outside these walls," she says. "Don't come in for anything. You're thinking I'm a crazy woman. This *mulata* knows, son. She knows what she's talking about. But listen to me this once. Don't, and I repeat DON'T get involved with what goes on here. For Chango's sake, take my advice."

Drawing one more puff from the cigar, she stands up and leaves the kitchen. He hears her in other rooms of the house. Though barefoot, she's got a heavy but quick footstep.

Now, after this interruption, he continues to work. As he scrapes, chips of paint jump from under the wire bristles of the brush and twirl down to the ground. He is almost finished with her window when he hears glass shatter next door.

III

THE crash came from another window, the one without a screen. The painter steps down the ladder carefully, holding onto the rungs, the steel scrape brush in his mouth. On the ground, he lifts the ladder and moves it—it bangs against and scratches the wall—and sets it firmly against the upstairs window.

He climbs to the window whose curtains are drawn shut, but whenever a slight breeze hits them and makes them billow, they part.

A man, his back to the window, outlined by the thin light shed from a reading lamp, stands facing the wall. He is wearing a coffee-stained undershirt which hugs a strong, corpulent torso, shoulders, and biceps.

The curtains block the painter's sight, but when they part again, the room is empty.

Water splashes from the bathroom and echoes in the bedroom where the bundled quilt, pillow and sheets cascade over the edge of the bed and droop over the cigarette-burnt rug. A crucifix stands on top of the scratched chiffonnier which is held up by bricks and milk crates.

Of all the windows, this one needs the least amount of scraping, and he gets the job done quickly. Termites have eaten little holes in the wood that he will have to seal with spackle, then prime and paint.

A slight tap on the infested part of the frame with the tip of the spatula and the wood cracks open to reveal the dugout tunnels. Empty arteries. Another tap uncovers a nest of eggs the size of pinheads, neatly tucked on the end of eaten wood.

"Hello up there," a voice says from below.

Underneath the ladder, he finds a small girl looking up at him.

"Hello down there," he says, looking down between the rungs of the ladder.

"What you doing?"

He's never seen anyone with a paler face, so wafer white, so round and pebble smooth in appearance.

"Scraping," the painter says. He comes down the ladder halfway.

"Scraping what?"

"Old paint."

"Um," she says, then looks down at her shoes. She pulls on the straps of her red corduroy dress. Her short, black hair is cropped evenly over her bushy eyebrows, and two long bangs curl in front of her ears. Once in a while, the little girl pushes the bangs behind her ears.

"Want to meet my brother Benny, um?" She pronounces her words slowly, carefully, as if she were chewing licorice or candy.

He tells her that he's too busy right now.

"Benny's your size. He's got a bigger stomach. Drinks beer, that's why. Do you drink beer, too?"

"Sometimes," he says. Yet beer is all he's been drinking lately, and he's glad it is beer and not liquor, for liquor gives him terrible hangovers.

"Benny smokes cigars."

The painter smokes cigarettes by the cartons.

"Yuck! I hate the smell." She puckers her lips and her cheeks fold inside her mouth.

Sounds of someone splashing water come from the pool, not visible from where he stands. The girl looks in its direction, then says, "You swim?"

"Sometimes." He grins, trying to hide his impatience.

"A man came and fixed the pool about two weeks ago."

"Marcia!" a woman's voice, which pronounces the name March-a, calls.

"Your mother's calling," he says.

"Dora's not my mother," Marcia says. She skips away and turns around the corner, out of sight.

Again on the ground, he lifts and carries the aluminum ladder to the other side of the building by the pool where he finds the young woman called Dora.

She stands on the edge of the diving board, ready for a backward somersault. The drops of water from her previous dive sparkle on her skin, then run down her tanned thighs to the whites of her feet.

She takes her time, stretches her slender arms skyward, then brings them down slowly to her side. Untanned half-moons of her breasts protrude from the edges of her suit as she pushes off the board. Her body bends in mid-air. Rotates. Bolts into the water.

Marcia, who rests her elbows on the railing at the top of the stairs, giggles and claps her hands. Behind her, thrown into silhouette by the screen door, stands a man the painter takes to be her brother Benny. He moves away from the door.

"That was great," Marcia says.

Dora swims underwater on her way back to the diving board. Looking at her, he pulls himself up the ladder one more time.

"Go inside," she tells Marcia, "and find out what your brother's up to."

"Up to no good," answers Marcia with such conviction that it makes Dora laugh.

Dora pulls herself out of the water and walks to a plastic chaise under the shade of a metal parasol. The shade makes her face darker, her green eyes glow. She sits, picks up the bottle of tanning lotion, uncaps it and squirts the oil on the palm of her hand. She starts to rub her arms, her abdomen, her thighs.

"Where did you learn to dive?" he asks her.

She rubs her arms and stomach, squints up at the roof and says, "Why?"

"You're good."

"Practiced a lot in school."

"Are you related to Marcia?" he asks.

"I babysit," she says. "Marcia and her brother. Their parents work late." She combs her wet hair back with her fingers. "When did Quiroga hire you?"

"You know him?" he asks.

"Sure."

"He hired me to paint."

"He better," she says and stands. She grabs the yellow towel hanging from the chaise's backrest and walks toward the downstairs apartment.

"He's a sneaky man," she says. She pulls the back of her suit over her buttocks.

"Look," he says, "he told me what he wants done and I'm going to do it."

"A sneaky son-of-a-bitch," she says, entering her apartment.

For a brief moment, the silence returns to the afternoon only to be disturbed by the painter's scraping and brushing off of peeled paint.

Marcia runs down the stairs from the upstairs apartment. "Where'd she go?"

He points.

Marcia knocks.

A voice tells her to come in, and she does, slamming the screen door shut.

He takes the brush and works on the window closest to the water's edge while making sure none of the scraped chips of paint fall into the pool.

IV

DURING the night, a warm breeze sweeps inside the hotel room. Tired from a long day of work, he tosses and turns, but fails to fall asleep. Sleep's been hard to get lately. Thoughts about his past come like the screams from the room next door.

Driven by nocturnal intrusions, he gets out of bed and moves in the dark looking for his cigarettes, which he feels for and finds on the dresser. He plucks one out of the pack, brings it to his dry lips and lights it.

Everywhere there are strange people, he thinks.

The dark swallows everything in the distance. Another moonless night here in the west. He wonders if the sun's coming up in the east. How long has he been at this end of the United States? So far from home—thousands of miles to be exact—never to return, not physically anyway, but through memories.

There was once an island, so blue, so beautiful. Distant. *Allá*, everybody called it. Over there. Sugarcane, cigars, women, fighting cocks and chameleons with long green tails, and games, the games of childhood: hopscotch, jump frog, *kimbumbia*, and stick ball ...

On the sidewalk beneath the firescape, a drunken old man holds on to the street lamp.

"*Chingada madre*," he swears while insects form a halo around the light. "*Órale, perros pendejos, déjenme tranquilo*," the old man says.

Here in this bedroom, the house painter thinks about the fears he once had about surviving.

The filthy clothes he wore at Mariel, he remembers, were all he arrived with. From Miami, he was taken to a camp in Pennsylvania where he was asked questions by immigration officials: Who was he? Name? Everybody has a name. Family lineage? What jobs, if any, did he perform in the old country? Did he serve in the armed forces? Was he a member of the secret police? Of the communist party? Sexual preference?

Once they cleared him—they liked the part about him running away from bootcamp—they returned him to Miami where he found work as a park attendant, and began to save a little money. Miami wasn't meant for him, he soon realized. The prejudices of his own people shocked him. Blacks were still not accepted. The people from Mariel were looked down upon. Nothing much had changed. The pre-revolutionary ways were preserved in Miami. So he said fuck them and came to California with aspirations of starting his own construction company. (He had done construction while serving in the military.) At first it was rough, since he didn't speak English, but Los Angeles was big enough to keep him occupied.

He throws the cigarette at the street and returns to the warm mattress where he finds little comfort, but nonetheless he lies down. A stomachache starts to take over his guts, twisting his intestines, knotting them. It feels like colic.

A mother argues with her child in the corridor.

"Fucking, God-forsaken place!" he mutters under his breath.

The sound of someone running up and down the hall sneaks inside the room. Voices, voices, broken into whispers behind walls.

"Hey, you!" a woman shouts. "You stop that right now, you hear me?"

"Stop it," a child screams. "Stop it! Stop it!"

A door slams shut and the slam makes the glass window behind the bed vibrate. The mother hits the boy and the sound of the last slap remains in the room long after she stops.

V

THE boy next door screams and the room fills with a shrill-like noise. In the dark, the painter hurries to the bathroom where he kneels over the toilet and vomits. Long tendrils of spittle hang from the corners of his mouth. He wipes them off with the back of his hand. He flushes the toilet, flips the light on, and squints at the disarray: the dark orange ring in the toilet, four or five cardboard toilet paper tubes twisted out of shape on top of the dirty clothes hamper, a filthy towel cornered under the sink to stop a leak, a rusty Gillette blade on top of an unused, but unwrapped bar of soap. Oh, the squalor! This is the way he's been living since he arrived in Los Angeles.

Hurrying, he showers for no other reason than to do something. He took a shower earlier, after he reheated and ate the leftovers that now upset his stomach. In the tub, he stands motionless and lets the spray of cold water fall over his head.

How long has he been living here? he wonders, having lost count of the months. When he first moved in he met some friends, Clara and Pineda, but they moved away last month because they didn't pay rent. Clara was a waitress and Pineda a busboy. They were a strange couple, but they often invited him to dinner or a glass of beer.

Anything to beat the loneliness.

By the time he finishes in the bathroom, it's five o'clock in the morning, the hour when the only sounds come from inanimate objects: the creaking of the floorboards, toilets gurgling, and water flowing inside pipes. He dresses for work in his overalls and goes downstairs to the lobby where he sits and reads the newspaper.

In the local section of *La Opinión* he spots the following headline: CUBAN REFUGEE COMMANDEERS ELEVATOR.

It is a story about a man who jams one of the elevators between floors at the Westin Bonaventure Hotel, holds hostage an old American couple from Montana who are vacationing in California. He demands to be flown back to Habana where he can be reunited with his family. He says he didn't want to come here, that he was forced. Three hours later, authorities bring in a woman who claims to know the man. She talks him into letting the couple go. Several hours later he does, then surrenders to a special police unit.

The article angers the painter. If he were in the man's position, he'd take the elevator all the way to the top floor, break the glass and jump. No need to take innocent people hostage.

He puts the paper down. His eyes burn from lack of sleep. Outside the dawn has dissolved into a grayish haze and the air feels cool, fresh and free of the usual smog.

A black man on a Cushman sidewalk sweeper, which zig-zags its way around the vagrants sleeping in the doorways, stares at him as he steps away from the entrance of the hotel. He walks to where the van is parked as the grinding noise of the brushes scrubbing the asphalt chases him away.

VI

A quick stop at the Winchell's on Alameda for coffee and donuts and already he begins to feel better. More energetic. Every morning breaks the same. It is as if each time he is born out of a cocoon in which he has been stricken with insomnia. His muscles need to warm up; his joints unhinge.

The morning begins to change. On the streets, traffic's backed up as far as the entrance to the freeway. To get to the building, he cuts through side streets and alleys. He drives the van up the driveway and parks it on the other side of the building, where he keeps the ladder chained to the inside of the fence.

He wastes no time setting up. On the roof he scrapes the paint off along the edges.

This is also the time of morning when all thoughts have left him alone. It becomes easier to concentrate, even on menial tasks.

Dora walks out of her apartment wearing a bikini. She goes to the diving board. Her hair is wet, and her feet leave wet prints on the cement. After she dives and swims the length of the pool, she notices him on the roof again.

"You get pleasure out of spying on people?" she says.

"I wasn't spying."

"What were you doing then?"

"Working, what does it look like I'm doing?"

"I have a million ideas," she says. She's kicking her feet underwater. "Always begin this early?"

"Whenever I can," he says.

She smiles and swims to the other side, submerges, pushes herself away from the tiles, and resurfaces. Her agility underwater is amazing.

"Your diving's excellent," he says.

"I practice once in a while. This diving board's cracked."

"I'll report it," he says. "Maybe Quiroga can have it fixed."

"Don't tell him anything, you understand? Someone came to fix the pool two weeks ago and I kicked him out. Quiroga was paying the bastard to keep an eye on me."

"Why would he do that?"

"Because I'm his girlfriend" she says, "and he's a very jealous man."

He hears the jingle of loose change. The manager walks by, pulling an empty shopping cart. She's humming a song. Dora ducks underwater and waits for the woman to pass.

When she comes back up he asks her where he might find the nearest pay phone.

"I'd let you use mine, but ... "

"I have to tell Quiroga to come and see the finished windows."

"See the windows," she says. She is now sitting on the edge, her hands behind her and her feet dangling in the water.

"I have to let him know."

"What's there to see? You've either finished them or you haven't, right?"

"I need an advance to buy the paint."

"What makes you think he'll give it to you?" she says.

"You seem to know him well," says the painter.

"Not well enough. Sometimes he surprises me."

"How long have you lived here?"

"Since the beginning of summer. I hate it here."

"It's going to look a lot nicer once I finish."

"Come down and use the phone," she says, getting out of the water. She sits on the chaise.

On the way around the building, he surprises a man leaning against the wall, looking at Dora. The man looks at the painter and smiles.

"The door's open," she says. "The phone's to your right as you enter."

"The man who lives next door to the manager was looking at you."

"Elias. He likes to watch me," she says.

"Who is he?"

"He's an ex-priest. He left the church a long time ago, when he left Cuba."

"After the Revolution?" he asks.

"That's when my parents took me out of the country," she says. "I was a year old."

He enters her apartment and finds the phone and dials. New furniture crowds the living room. A chrome lamp extends in an arch from behind the plush sofa, over the matching glass centertable. Cornered on the other side of the room, a big screen television faces the sofa and chairs. Every object is neatly placed, giving the room an air of luxury.

No one answers, so he hangs up. Dora comes in and closes the door.

Everything is so clean, he thinks, maybe Quiroga pays a cleaning woman to come and ...

"Not there?" she says, drying her hair with the towel.

"His secretary's not answering. I'll try later," he says.

"Do you have his home number?"

"No, he didn't give it to me. I guess he doesn't want to be bothered at home."

"Is that what he said?"

"That's what I think he meant."

"Want coffee?"

He tells her not to bother, that he must return to the roof.

"No bother, it's made." She steps into the kitchen. Moments later she returns with two coffee mugs, hands him one. He avoids staring at her breasts.

"Nice furniture," he says, realizing that his weak tone of voice betrays his sincerity. He becomes self-conscious because he is only trying to make conversation.

"Tell me the truth," she says, "is this what you really do, paint?"

"Yes."

Silence.

He asks, "Are your parents here in California?"

"My father died. My mother lives in Miami."

The coffee tastes bitter, but he drinks it anyway. "I left my parents in Habana."

"You came recently?"

Soon it will be two years since he arrived, he tells Dora.

"At least," she says, "you're better off than some others. Not all like to work, you know. *Marielitos* have given the established Cuban community a bad name."

"I like to work," he says. Work has kept him going, stable. He recalls the article in this morning's newspaper. "What you say about *Marielitos* isn't true."

She ignores his last statement, then says, "And work's what you're here to do, right?"

He thanks Dora for the coffee and tells her that he'll try to reach Quiroga later. She gives him a suspicious, indifferent look.

Outside, he greets Marcia who is playing in the pool. Upstairs, Benny stands peering down at him. Benny's face is dark, hair combed to the side. A bushy, well-groomed mustache.

After the painter climbs to the roof and continues with his work, Benny comes down the stairs, knocks on Dora's door and enters her apartment.

VII

SOON all the windows are scraped, holes and gaps sealed with spackle, primed and masked. The work goes fast, uninterrupted. He buys the supplies with his own money. Waiting for Quiroga to show up, he sweeps debris of paint and pieces of masking tape into small mounds by Dora's open bedroom window and looks in.

There's a loud knock at her front door. Dora walks out of the bathroom wrapped in a black silk robe which comes undone, exposing her breasts and pubic hair. The front door's not visible from where he is looking in.

Sound of a door being unlocked.

"Perfect for this table," she says.

"Glad you like them," a man says.

The man with his back to the window turns and the painter recognizes Quiroga's face.

"Adore flowers," she says to Quiroga. Dora drops her robe as Quiroga embraces her and buries his face between her neck and shoulders.

"Benny won't bother us today, will he?" Quiroga says.

"He doesn't mean to intrude."

"Inopportune's more his style. I don't like the way he drools every time he sees you."

"He doesn't drool," she says, moving away from Quiroga.

"Doesn't do the things you'd expect someone with his problem to—"

"Leave him alone," she says and walks into the bedroom. The painter ducks out of the way just in time, for she almost catches him.

"Been keeping yourself busy?" Quiroga asks. He follows Dora into the bedroom, stands by her dresser, and unbuttons his shirt.

While Dora goes in to the bathroom, Quiroga searches

over the surface of the dresser as if looking for clues, anything that will reveal her unfaithfulness.

"Trying," she says, returning to the bedroom. She sits
on the bed, then says, "I met the guy you hired to paint."

"The *Marielito*?" Quiroga's voice sounds gritty. "Is he
doing a good job?"

"You hired him to ... to keep ... is he keeping an eye
on me?"

Quiroga says no, he'd never hire anybody to spy on her.
His jealousy, he says, is only proof of how much he loves
her.

"And you never paid Candelaria to watch over me?"

"She hates you," he says.

"Tell me what he's doing here?"

"I told you. Working."

"I don't like the way he looks at me," she says.

"Probably finds you attractive," Quiroga says. "Who
wouldn't? All you do's sunbathe in those skimpy ... these
Marielitos are so horny."

"I'm bored here. I hate it."

"I hired him to turn this place into a palace. Your
palace."

"Flattery isn't going to get you between my legs."

"Let's not argue, okay?"

Dora gets on her hands and knees while Quiroga strad-
dles her from behind.

"And that fence," she says. "I hate it. Knock it down."

"Protection." Quiroga holds onto her waist and rocks
faster. The springs in the mattress sound their complaints.

"Protection my ass," she says, "you're keeping me
locked up. I can't go anywhere without you finding out."

Now the bed stops moving and the painter hears their
heavy breathing slow down. He wants to look, but the
thought that he might lose his job if Quiroga sees him
keeps him from doing so.

Quiroga groans. They finish, so Quiroga sits up on the edge of the bed and lights a cigarette. Dora covers herself with the bedsheet and rolls away from Quiroga.

"Has Elias bothered you again?" he says.

"You think everyone bothers me."

"One of these days I'm going to evict his ass."

"Temper, temper," she says. "You're going to end up evicting everyone." Dora laughs.

"Including you, smartass," Quiroga says. He combs his hair back and stretches his arms out in front of him as if to check for scratches or bruises.

"I don't need any notices."

"You won't get any."

The painter peeps in and sees Quiroga, who's got his fat, hairy hands on Dora's breasts, trying to get on top of her.

"You make it sound like I'm fucking everyone in this building," she says, "and I don't like it."

"Put up with it," Quiroga says. "I don't trust Elias."

"What could he offer me? He's a priest."

"Was a priest."

Quiroga walks around the bed putting his clothes back on. Once in a while he looks in the dresser mirror to check his hair.

"I need money," Dora says.

Quiroga asks how much.

"I don't know. Five, six hundred."

"I don't have that kind of cash with me right now."

"*She* would make you go to the bank and get it."

"Leave her out of it," he says.

"Does your wife have to fuck you to get—"

"Enough!"

Dora gets out of bed and walks to the bathroom. The painter hurries to the front of the building where he sweeps and waits for Quiroga to come out.

Benny appears and stands by the doorway. When Quiroga walks out, he bumps into him. The blue in Benny's scared, beady eyes brings a wild look to his face. Quiroga pushes Benny out of the way.

With beads of sweat on his reddened forehead, Quiroga walks around the pool and approaches the painter. "Show me what you've done," he says.

He leads the boss around the building. Quiroga inspects the first window he comes to by lifting the masking tape and running his fingers over the primed wood.

The painter tells him he plans to start painting tomorrow, but that he can't do so until he has enough money to buy ten gallons of paint.

"That's going to cover ... ?" he asks.

"Front building," says the painter.

"All I have on me's seventy dollars," he says. "Is that enough?"

"That'll buy five gallons," he says. "You owe me for the spackle and primer."

"Keep a tab, okay?"

Leaving the money on the windowsill, Quiroga turns and walks to the parking lot. He watches as Quiroga gets into his Cadillac and drives away from the curb.

When the painter returns to the back, Marcia is standing knee deep in the pool.

"Do you want to swim?" she asks.

"Not right now."

Dora comes out of the apartment, walks over to the diving board, and dives in.

He begins to sweep up what's left of the paint and tape. The sun dips behind the building, leaving behind a red-orange glow.

VIII

LATER that week, Quiroga, clad in crisp new designer clothes more appropriate for a younger man, asks the painter to have lunch with him. There are important business matters to discuss between them. Something bothers the painter about his boss; Quiroga can't look anybody straight in the eyes.

On the way, nothing much is said between them.

The leather interior of the car makes him feel warm and comfortable. SEVILLE, the gold letters on the wood dashboard read.

El Ranchito is a Mexican restaurant which, according to Quiroga, serves the best food in town. He eats there often. As the Cadillac pulls into the parking lot, a boy appears out of nowhere and taps on the windshield. The boy's clothes are tattered; his skin is a deep, sunburnt brown.

"Please, *señor*," he says, "clean your glass?"

Quiroga ignores the boy and turns into a parking space. The boy stands and waits.

"These Mexicans," Quiroga says, "they're going to turn this city into another Tijuana."

Climbing out of the car, he tells the boy to get away from the car. If he returns and finds so much as a smudge, he's going to call the police.

The boy and Quiroga exchange glances, then the boy spits and walks away to seek shelter from the sun under the shade of the red, white and green canvas awning.

A mural of an Aztec warrior holding a woman in his arms on top of a mountain adorns the entrance of the restaurant. On closer inspection, the brush strokes appear to have been laid on in a thick, criss-cross fashion.

A Mexican waiter greets both men as they walk in. He salutes Quiroga, then asks them to follow. Leading them to a table in the back, he waits for them to sit down, then hands over the menus to the *caballeros.*

Quiroga puts his glasses on the crooked bridge of his nose and opens the menu. The waiter returns with a basketful of tortilla chips and hot sauce.

"What will you have, *señores?*" the waiter asks.

Quiroga orders the chicken fajitas and the painter orders a burrito special. The waiter collects the menus and leaves.

Silence.

Then, Quiroga says, "Making great progress?"

"Moving along."

"Those apartments are going to look beautiful."

"I'll try to finish quickly," the painter says.

"Don't rush," he says. Quiroga picks a couple of chips out of the basket and dips them into the red sauce. When he bites into them, which he does fiercely, the crunch of the corn tortillas is loud.

The painter tells his boss how he's met most of the tenants in the apartment complex. Quiroga's eyes widen as he stares at his employee from behind his glasses.

"You met Candelaria?" Quiroga says. "I'm afraid she's a little on the other side, you know what I mean?" He smiles, then says, "I think I can offer you the chance to prosper. I plan to buy more buildings in need of repair. I've bid on two already. They're not too far from this area. Both need a lot of work."

"The more work the better," says the painter.

"Where are you living?"

"Hotel."

"Tell you what," Quiroga says, "for the time being, why don't you stay in one of the apartments. Tell Candelaria to show them to you. Pick the one you like. You can live in it rent free."

The painter eats a couple of chips dipped in hot sauce

which immediately set his mouth on fire. It is the spicy food he'll remember later, he thinks, not the company nor the conversation.

"All you've got to do's continue fixing the building," Quiroga says, then lowers his voice. "Look, I'm a married man but my wife and I don't ... you understand? I met this young woman in Miami and brought her here."

"Dora?" asks the painter. "The good-looking one who's always wearing those bikinis?"

The boss's eyes narrow, grow cold, then, "The same," he says. "She's my ... she's young, you know and needs attention."

"How young?" The painter drinks an entire glass of water to cool his mouth, but to no use in abating the flaming sensation.

"I want you to keep an eye on her, but don't make it too obvious."

The painter takes his cloth napkin and spreads it open over his lap. "I'm going to need furniture."

"We'll work something out," Quiroga says matter of factly, as if this had been something he'd thought of and planned for a long time.

"I want the place to look nice."

"Keep working on the building, watch Dora, keep track of who she talks to. Let me know if anyone visits. And I'll give you a bonus to get you that furniture."

"Don't you think that if she really wanted to, if she set her mind on sneaking about, she could get away with it?"

Quiroga composes himself, smiles and turns his attention to the tortilla chips.

"When can I move in?" the painter wants to know.

"That's up to you," he says. "Just ask Candelaria for the key."

The food arrives hot, swirls of steam rise toward the ceiling. Quiroga calls the guitar player over to the table and asks him to play "*Guantanamera.*"

It is an upbeat, twangy rendition.

After lunch they walk back to the car, the painter feeling the fullness of his stomach. The boy who wanted to clean the windshield squats on his heels. He spits again and looks away in the opposite direction.

IX

SATURDAY morning, he wastes no time in gathering his cardboard-bound suitcase full of unwashed clothes, a couple of boxes and a small mattress. He throws everything into the back of the van and drives away.

He drives up and parks in front of the apartments. Indeed, after what little cosmetic work he's done, in *coup d'état* fashion, the whole complex looks better, more pleasant, on its way to regaining the grandeur it once possessed.

He knocks.

Candelaria, sleepy-eyed, face unwashed, and wearing a man's robe, answers the door. She holds on to the knob as if to steady herself.

"Show me some of the apartments," he says. He stands in front of her, determined. No matter what she tells him, he's still moving in.

"This early in the fucking morning?" she says, wiping the sleepcrusties from the corners of her eyes.

He apologizes for waking her up, but he wants an early start. Sunday he will rest, then continue with work the following day.

She goes inside and leaves the door open a crack. He waits by the stairs. Candelaria returns wearing slippers and a *mantilla* wrapped around her shoulders.

He tells her he'd prefer one upstairs. Hers is the only two-story apartment in the complex.

Up the stairs, he follows Candelaria quietly.

"Up here's more expensive," she says, "because of the extra bathroom."

"I'm not paying rent," he says, wondering how much breeze will blow into the rooms.

She stops short of the last step and turns around to look at him. "What did he ask you to do for him?" she says.

"It isn't a favor," he says.

"Still don't know what you're getting into, do you?"

"He hired me to paint," he answers, "and I paint."

"To paint."

"This one and two other buildings."

"And for that," she says, "not only is he paying you, but he's letting you live rent free."

"Got it." He points to the corner apartment and tells her he'd like to see it.

"Elias lives there," she says.

"How about the one next to his?"

She searches for the key on her key ring, finds it, and unlocks the door. He steps into the unfurnished apartment and finds that the walls are badly cracked and the wood floors scratched and dull.

"All interiors look the same," she says.

"Everything can be fixed," he says and walks around the place contemplating the possibilities.

"When do you plan to move in?"

"Immediately."

"It's too late to stop you," she says, "so suit yourself."

He walks into another room and leaves Candelaria by the front door. When he returns, she's no longer there. She's left the key in the lock.

X

STRETCHED on his bed with a pillow folded under his neck, Benny smokes a cigar while throwing a tennis ball against the ceiling of his room.

The painter stands on the ladder outside the boy's window and watches how the ball slices through the smoke hovering over the bed. Benny talks to himself while the painter finishes masking the window.

"I hate him, that bastard. Elias tells me to watch. Watch out for when the son-of-a-bitch leaves. Elias and Dora spend a lot of time together. I don't like it when Elias tells me to leave him and Dora alone, to go stand outside just in case Quiroga returns. I don't like it when Dora's alone with Elias. I hate being on the lookout."

"Benny," a voice says, "are you in there?"

Benny springs from the bed, rushes to the dresser, takes a can of Lysol out of the first drawer and sprays frantically all around his bed. He opens the door. Marcia steps in and says Dora wants to see him downstairs.

She sniffs the air. "Ooh," she says, "you've been smoking in here again."

Benny shakes his head.

"I smell it."

"That's not what you think you smell," he says.

"Liar," Marcia says.

"Honest," he says.

Marcia stands by the dresser with her arms crossed.

"Oh," Benny says, "please don't tell mom."

She tells him she doesn't know if she will or won't, then turns around and buzzes out of the room. Pleading, Benny storms after her.

XI

RAIN falls for the next couple of days. Deluge fashion. The painter stands behind his living room window and watches the rain saturate the earth. Fallen leaves cover the ground and rot in muddy puddles. Worms leave the grassy patches for the cemented walkways. After the rain, when the sun comes out and the puddles begin to dry in the heat, the worms perish.

Quiroga has been away on a business trip—so his secretary reveals. Work can't continue until the rain stops and the walls dry.

Barefoot, the painter moves through the different rooms in the apartment, listening to the silence, the soft buzzing. The rain falls so hard it reminds him of home, of things he'd rather not think about.

Later in the morning, Elias walks out of Dora's apartment. Wet hair, deep-set tired eyes. Moving around the pool, Elias looks up and sees the painter.

Before he will tell Quiroga the truth about Dora and Elias, he will demand more money. So is the nature of the game.

XII

SATURDAY afternoon Candelaria sends Elias up to the painter's apartment to invite him to dinner, a sort of welcoming. Elias, dressed in faded blue jeans and a white *guayabera*, asks if he needs help with anything, moving stuff around. "Two extra hands never hurt," says Elias.

The painter thanks Elias for offering to help, but the rain has given the painter a chance to arrange his belongings and fix a few odds and ends.

Elias slides his white hands into his pockets and leans against the door frame. The painter invites him to come in and sit down.

Elias is tall and thin, flabby around the waist. He's got strong arms, and a hairless, reddish chest. What appeals to the painter about this man's looks are the freckles. Bunches of them stand out on his face and forearms. If anything, Elias hardly seems the type of man to have been a priest. A bricklayer, yes, but not a member of the clergy.

"Dora tells me you came from Mariel," he says.

"That's right," the painter says, "and she told me you were a priest."

The painter sits down on the floor across from where Elias stands.

"I left the church after the Revolution," he says. "Times were hard. I left Cuba in 1970 and went to Madrid."

"What made you stop being a priest?" asks the painter.

"I found out that I didn't get along with people the way a priest should. To devote yourself you must have the right—how can I say it—attitude. Which I didn't have."

"You still believe?"

Elias smiles and looks down at his tennis shoes. "Still," he says.

"Leave any family behind when you left?" the painter asks.

"My parents died long ago."

Elias's large, droopy eyes are those of a man too familiar with human despair, with grief and agony.

"Quiroga likes you," he says, then grows pensive. "The building needs a lot of fixing."

"Monday I start painting."

"Listen," he says, "I know you saw me walk out of Dora's apartment."

"That's none of my business," the painter says, as if to put the man at ease.

"I met her when she moved in. Candelaria introduced us. We used to talk a lot about diving—something she should pursue. Whenever Quiroga wasn't around, we'd spend most of our time together."

"She's his mistress."

Elias's face grows stern as though he's been insulted by the painter's boldness. "That's all going to change one day," he says.

"You love her?"

"Very much," he says. "I'll be honest with you. Right now I'm broke, so she's been helping me out financially."

Elias reveals that Dora's father died and that her mother's an alcoholic. Dora met Quiroga during a time when she did things to hurt her mother. Out of spite. One day she moved out here with him, and for a while she believed she loved him.

"She doesn't any more," he says.

The painter remembers when he saw Dora and Quiroga in bed fornicating.

"Despises him now," Elias adds. He stands and, moving toward the door, tells the painter not to forget about dinner. "Candelaria's a wonderful cook," he says.

A voice calls Elias from downstairs. Although the person calling cannot be seen, the voice sounds familiar, and the painter figures it must be Dora. Elias goes down, then the painter sees him and Dora walk away together.

XIII

CANDELARIA peels two plantains with a sharp knife, splits them in half, pokes holes into them with a fork, and finally sprinkles brown sugar all over them. On the plate, the plantains look like the open hands of a woman praying. He observes as she takes butter, melts it in a tin cup over the stove, and lets it drip over the plantains.

"You know why these are called drunken plantains?" she says, licking the butter off her fingers. "Because you take this—" She opens the cupboards and reaches up for a bottle of dark rum. "And you drown the bastards in this holy juice."

Once finished she takes a swig, caps the bottle, and places it on the kitchen table.

"That's that," she says, "but the *arroz con pollo* has a while to go. Let's go sit down."

Bacardi in hand, she leads the way out of the kitchen to the living room downstairs. There she mixes a couple of Cuba Libres and she and the painter sit down to drink.

"I thought Elias was going to be here?" he asks.

"Uh-uh," she says. "He went out with you know who."

"You don't like her much, do you?"

"Now, now," she says. "Look into my eyes." She opens them wide. "See any hatred?"

He sees lot's of it, but he doesn't tell her.

"I don't hate her," she says, taking a sip of her drink. "I abhor that little *puta*."

This is going to be open warfare, he says to himself, sinking deeper and deeper into the cushions on the sofa. On an empty stomach, the rum tastes hot.

"Quiroga brings her to me," she says, "and asks me to take care of her. From minute one she and I didn't like each other. We argued. At the time I was taking care of Benny and Marcia. Before I knew it, Dora took over.

Marcia's mother came and talked to me, told me it'd be better if Marcia had somebody younger, like Dora, to take care of Marcia. Someone Marcia could relate to.

"I lost a good eighty dollars a week. All because of her. She's a snake, that's what she is. She manages to charm everybody she meets. I don't know how she does it, but she does. That's why I tried to warn you. She can do a number on you."

"I can take care," he says without emotion.

"Same thing I heard Elias say once," she says.

Her drink's gone, and she stands up to mix another. Sweat covers her forehead and upper lip.

"Quiroga," she starts again, "the poor fool. He thinks he's got this young pussy under control, you know. He comes and goes. Fucks her all the time, I imagine. And goes. He doesn't care. What he's afraid of is that she might hurt his pride. Hell, he's got a wife. Kids Dora's age. I'm glad all this is happening. Fuck her. Fuck him."

"And Elias," he says, "is involved?"

"If I were him," she says, "I'd wet my dick and go about my business. But no. The damn fool goes and falls in love."

Three drinks later they still haven't had dinner. His stomach feels hollow, as though someone has taken a shovel and dug his guts out. Candelaria's on her way to drunkenness, if she isn't there already. After her fourth drink, she brings the bottles of rum and coke over and sets them on the floor between her legs.

"*¡Hijo de la gran puta!*" she says. "That's what Quiroga is."

"Maybe we should go up."

"You'd never believe me if I told you something."

He stands up and moves the bottles out of her way.

"I used to be his lover," she says, and finishes the last of her drink. "Damn right. Years ago when these," she grabs her breasts, "were nice and firm, I used to wear him out, that man, go at his dick with a vengeance."

"I smell something burning," the painter says with enough urgency in his voice to make her believe it.

Candelaria stands up, sets her empty glass on the arm of the sofa, and hurries upstairs to the kitchen. He follows her and when he arrives, the chicken and rice are ready on the table.

"It looks great," he says.

She removes the plantains from the oven and pushes some of it onto a plate. "Enjoy," she says.

He attacks the food in a way he's never eaten before. Candelaria sits in front of him and leaves her plate untouched. Instead of eating, she takes another bottle of rum from under the kitchen sink and sits back down to drink it.

Without saying a word, the painter raises his glass to propose a toast, but in the end nothing is said. Candelaria reaches over, her white teeth showing behind fleshy, wet lips, and taps his glass with hers.

XIV

LOUD noises awake him. At first he thinks it's the train passing, but when he sits up and looks out the window, he sees Candelaria sitting on the edge of the diving board.

She is soaked, legs kicking at the water. It is three-thirty in the morning, and she's drunk. She's saying things he hears but can't understand. Instead of going back to sleep, he puts on a pair of shorts, finds his slippers, and goes downstairs.

"My lovely, lovely," she says to him as he approaches. "Come to make love, eh?"

He tells her to keep her voice down or half the neighborhood will wake up. Her breath smells sweetly of rum.

"Who are you?" she says.

"Let's go inside," he tells her, reaching over to take her hand.

"Don't touch me!"

"You'll fall and hurt yourself, Candelaria."

"If you touch me I'll jump in."

"Go ahead, then, jump."

She tries to stand, but can't. "Here I go," she says.

He moves over to her quickly, grabs her, and pulls her away from the edge. She's strong, feisty, and with a hard firm grip, she claws at his forearms. She's like a cat.

"I said get your hands off," she says.

He carries her back to her apartment, pushes the door open with his foot, and takes her inside. Her clothes are too wet to put her on the sofa, but he does it anyway.

"Goddamn you," she says, "I was waiting for him."

"Who?"

"I'm going to kill that son-of-a-bitch."

After tucking a cushion under her head, he stands back. "Where can I get you a blanket?" he asks.

"Go away," she says. "Leave me alone."

In the vestibule, he finds an old coat which he takes and throws over Candelaria. She's fallen asleep.

On the way back to his apartment, Elias's door opens and Dora walks out. The painter hides in the shadows. They stand close, embrace and kiss. Dora walks away and Elias goes back inside. Then the painter goes up the stairs and enters the apartment.

In bed he smokes one cigarette, then another. A siren fades away in the distance. The train passes a bit later and its horn echoes in the dark of the room. Airplanes fly overhead. He falls asleep shortly before dawn.

XV

THROUGH a crack on one of the boards in the attic, he sees them, follows their every movement, the G-2's, secret police. They have come for him. He hides in the attic of his parents' house in Habana. The two policemen stand by the gate, chainsmoking while they wait. They've come to take him back to the camp from which he escaped.

There they are, their mouths moving, their hands gesturing, but he cannot hear what they're saying to each other. The worst that can happen once they find him is that they'll send him to Angola or some other place in the dark continent.

A joke comes to him as he sits watching, waiting for them to leave. What's the best thing to tell a mother when her son dies in some muddy trench, his body blown into a million unrecognizable pieces? That her son deserted and is now in Miami.

In the attic he hides for several days, each morning awakened by their loud knocking on the front door. His mother comes out. Looking down on her, she looks small, her unkempt hair combed back in a hurry. She is wearing one of the old man's robes with no belt so she has to keep her hands at her bosom.

Where is he? the taller of the two asks.

Not here, his mother says. Go away, please, go away. He's not here.

Your son should know better than to run away, the other man says. Tell him that when you see him.

She closes the door on them. The G-2s go away only to return to the front gate minutes later. They light new cigarettes. They won't give up and neither will he.

When the break-in at the Peruvian Embassy in Miramar occurs, he sneaks out one night and goes there.

From the embassy, everyone is bussed to the port of

Mariel and shipped out to Miami. What chaos! But there is nothing like freedom, at last.

XVI

"ALL this time," Quiroga, whose face is suntanned, says, "and you haven't seen anything?"

The painter lies. The only person he's seen go in and out of Dora's apartment, he says, has been Dora herself. "And Marcia," he adds.

Quiroga is sitting inside his car dressed in a three-piece, grey flannel suit which seems to be uncomfortable by the way he keeps moving. The knot of his striped tie, too thick under his chin, looks as though it is choking him.

"As you can see," the painter continues, pointing toward the front of the building, "the paint's coming along."

Quiroga looks at his employee and doesn't say anything. With his thick hands, he wipes the back of his neck.

Moments of silence. A group of kids walks by with a large radio. They are singing along with the music.

The noise fades, then silence.

"The rain slowed me down a bit."

"Keep an eye open," Quiroga says, then puts the car in gear and speeds off.

Dressed in his paint-spattered overalls, the painter stands on the sidewalk and watches the boss go until the Cadillac turns and disappears at the corner.

XVII

ALL the stains and cracks disappear from the walls as he rolls the paint on, working around the masked windows. And before the week's over, the entire front facade of the building is finished. A world of difference, he thinks, becoming more proud of the work with each finished section.

Listening to a portable radio in Candelaria's window during one of his paint-fast-and-get-the-hell-out-of-here sprees, he hears a report about *Marielitos*. They are being arrested by the dozens and put in jail. According to authorities, they've gone crazy, they can't cope with the fast life in the U.S.A. Of those left who haven't killed themselves or turned to alcohol or drugs, their souls have died, or they've committed themselves to petty crimes. Credit card fraud. Petty theft. Burglary. Gambling. Once arrested and put in high-security prisons, they burn their cell mattresses and pillows in protest.

" ... most have visible tattoos," the voice of the interviewed official says. "Cuban prison numbers marked on the inside of the bottom lip."

Candelaria enters her kitchen and he asks her to please turn the radio off. She seems to be in a better mood, as if what occurred the night she cooked dinner is forgotten, thrown over the abyss of her memory.

"Listen to music," she says.

"No music," he says and rolls the paint.

XVIII

MARCIA runs up to tell him that Dora and Candelaria are arguing. Their shouts startle him. He stops working and runs to the patio.

"Whore!" Candelaria screams.

"It takes one to know one," Dora says. She waves a towel at Candelaria's face.

"Think you can piss on everybody, don't you? Well, you can't. Not on this *mulata*."

Dora turns around and moves toward her apartment door. Candelaria follows her there.

"Get out," Candelaria says.

"Woman, your ass's going to be on the street. Count on it."

"What are you going to do? Fuck him? Convince him to kick me out?"

"Oh," Dora says, "I don't care what happens."

Marcia climbs the stairs and waits by the veranda.

"He knows better," Candelaria says. Her eyes widen in their dark hollows.

"Mind your business," Dora says. "What Elias and I do's none of your goddamned business, so keep your nose out!"

Benny appears on the balcony. He is smoking a cigar. "Shut up!" he screams. Marcia pushes him back inside and closes the door.

"You are using Elias," Candelaria says.

Dora steps inside.

Candelaria bends over, bracelets jingling, picks up a handful of dirt, and throws it at the screen door.

"Witch!" Marcia calls to Candelaria, and slams the door as she enters her apartment.

"You're going to grow up and be just like her," Candelaria says, then sees the painter standing by the corner of the building, wet roller in hand, on the other side of the pool. She stares at him, then begins to walk away. He catches up and walks next to her.

"Jesus," he says, "what was that all about?"

"I'm tired," she says. "I'm leaving."

"Calm down."

Candelaria stops and puts her hand on his shoulder. "I'd get out too, quickly," she tells him.

"I'm not going anywhere," he says.

"Marcia came and told me Elias and Dora are moving out. They're going to do it," she says, "today or tomorrow."

"Quiroga doesn't know?"

"Going away somewhere," she says. "And I told Elias, warned him not to fool around with that bitch. I don't want Elias getting hurt," she says, "and she's bound to hurt him."

"Elias can take care of himself."

She casts a long, harsh stare at him, then says, "According to you, everybody can take care of themselves."

"Survival," he says as she walks away and leaves him alone there. It is something he knows a lot about: Survival!

XIX

IN his dreams, Dora's dressed in a silk, see-through gown. Her breasts and nipples show under it. She is leading him up the stairs, to the apartment. She opens the door and lets him in.

He walks in and sees all the new furniture in his apartment. The big screen television set, the stereo system, the sofa and matching chairs, all the chrome of the lamps and center table glows under the bright light, and, as he steps in, he feels the softness of the new shag carpet.

All yours, Dora says, this is all yours.

She removes her gown and approaches him on the sofa. Undressing him, she kisses him and her lips taste bitter.

Enjoy, she whispers into his ear.

Once naked, they begin to make love until he comes and the feeling leaves him spent.

XX

SILENCE becomes as common as the daily afternoon breeze that lifts and drags the dead leaves across the cemented patio. The painter takes advantage of the tranquility and gets most of the painting on the back building done.

All is fine until the morning he sees Quiroga drive up and park the car. The serious look on his face reveals what the boss has come for.

The painter avoids him; he prefers not to be the first person Quiroga encounters.

He is dressed casually, designer jeans and a Hawaiian print shirt. His steps are sure but slow as he moves between the hedged shrubs on his way to Dora's.

Once he enters, the painter makes his way around the building to the back where he hopes to find one of the windows open. None of them are, but the last one doesn't have its curtains shut. He can see Dora and Quiroga in the living room. They seem to be arguing.

Her face is calm, relaxed while Quiroga's is angered, red with fury.

The painter goes to the front where he might be able to hear something.

"I want that son-of-a-bitch out of here!" Quiroga's voice, though muffled behind the walls and closed windows, becomes audible, like the rumble of distant thunder.

"I'm going with him!" Dora yells back.

"Hell you are," Quiroga says and leaves.

Dora follows him outside.

"You bastard, son-of-a-bitch!" she yells at his back.

Benny, who apparently has been watching out for Quiroga, descends the stairs and approaches him. "Leave her alone," Benny says to him.

"Benny, go back upstairs!" Dora says.

Benny pushes Quiroga to get him to move back.

"Dora," Quiroga says, "get this idiot away from me before I hurt him."

"I'm not an idiot," Benny says and hits Quiroga on the chest.

Elias walks up from behind and embraces Quiroga before he strikes Benny. "Leave Benny alone," Elias says.

"Let go!" Quiroga yells.

"Elias, don't get involved!" Dora says.

"Whore," Quiroga says to Dora, trying to break free.

"She's coming with me," Elias tells him and lets go. "We're out of here."

"No, no, no!" Benny screams. He jumps on Quiroga and with a rock, bangs on his head and back. Blood runs out of a gash on Quiroga's scalp right above his left ear.

Quiroga turns around and jabs Benny square on the jaw and knocks him down on the grass.

Dora runs to Benny.

Elias fights with Quiroga, but Quiroga overpowers Elias and lands a blow on the side of Elias's head, rendering him unconscious.

The painter watches Quiroga approach Dora and start to slap her. She's not fighting back. Each slap sounds like a piece of wood snapping. A dark red-colored spot appears at the corner of Dora's swollen lips.

"Stop!" the painter says finally.

Quiroga keeps on hitting her. They are close to the edge of the pool.

He hurries to Quiroga and hits him with the paint roller behind the neck. Out of control now, wild, Quiroga won't stop. Can't stop.

Finally, the painter gets in the way and pushes Dora out from Quiroga's reach, but now Quiroga starts hitting the painter. Quiroga's fists pound on his flesh like a jackhammer. He never imagined Quiroga to be this quick and strong. With each exchange of punches, they move closer and closer to the edge of the water. Quick jabs in search of Quiroga's jaw are what the painter fights back with. He pushes Quiroga into the pool, hoping that the water will cool him off or slow him down or both, but Quiroga grabs hold of the painter's overall straps and pulls him in.

This is the deep end. The cool water tickles his skin. Quiroga's hands find his neck; his hands, Quiroga's eyes. They struggle and go under. The painter thinks he can hear Dora's voice begging them to stop.

For a brief moment all he can think about are Candelaria's eyes. They are peering down at him, bloodshot and wide open.

He is swallowing a lot of water. After a while he can't tell if Quiroga's hands are still holding him down. Something's certainly pulling the painter down, down, and it feels like it's never going to let go.

Dearly Beloved

1.

PILAR sat in her corner of the worn divan sipping her coffee so as not to burn her tongue. She watched *El Maldito*, the eight o'clock soap opera on channel 34.

Armando sat quietly at the other end, waiting for Julia, his wife, who had left moments before to buy a pizza, another item on her endless list of cravings. He understood that now that she was pregnant she was eating for two. The I-will-be-back-soon prolonged into what seemed hours as he sat alone with his mother-in-law in the stuffy living room of the old house. Julia had left, he concluded, so that her mother and he could reconcile and speak to one another. This was his first visit to the house since he and Julia had got back together.

After Gustavo, Pilar's husband, had left, the house looked messy, unkempt, like a house in the process of being remodeled or moved into. The dim lamp shed light upon the film of dust on the television console, lamp table, picture frames and coffee table under which the last issue of the telephone directory lay yellowed, untouched. The room smelled of soiled rags and fried fish, when it had at one time smelled of lilac or rose water air freshener.

2.

Steam whirled from the porcelain mug to Pilar's eyes and forehead. She sat with her shoulders bent forward, her large breasts under her blue robe spilled over her stomach. She blinked to the changing pictures on the screen. The sound of rusty, static voices coming from the console's side speaker muffled the silence.

The face of an old woman appeared on the screen. Her voice, when she spoke, carried the metallic sound of make-believe despair. A soft crackle. She seemed like an old woman who at the end of her life struggles, with afflictions of sickness and solitude, to endure her suffering a little longer.

3.

"I'm worried," Armando said. "She shouldn't have gone out in this weather."

"Julia can take care of herself," Pilar said, not turning from the screen.

Julia, he knew better than anyone else, was a poor driver. She drove like a crazy person: made left turns without signalling, changed from lane to lane, and tried to beat the traffic lights before they turned red.

4.

Pilar had put on extra pounds since the last time he saw her, two or three months after his separation from her daughter. As she had walked through the sliding door of El Pueblo Market, she had spotted him getting out of his car. Maricela, one of the women he had dated, was with him. Pilar gave her a harsh, cold stare. Embarrassed, he turned and headed straight for the IN door. Minutes later he walked out puzzled—Maricela had followed him in and out—having completely forgotten what he had gone to buy.

Pilar looked at him through the steam as though she knew what he was thinking. He knew that she hadn't forgotten the incident. Maricela had dismissed his distraction as just another one of his absent-minded acts.

5.

A couple kissed in a Colgate toothpaste commercial.

"How much longer?" Armando asked, staring at Pilar's shiny mug. All this time had passed and she hadn't offered him any coffee.

She said she didn't know, then peeled her fingers one at a time from around the mug as she regripped the handle.

"Cornelli's isn't that far."

"She must have gone somewhere else."

A moment of silence followed in which he could hear the soft rattle of the heater's fan.

6.

"How can you watch that, Pilar?"

She turned from the screen. "It's the only thing I watch."

"Watch the American channels. They have variety."

"I see nothing wrong with this."

What he wanted to say, to confess, was that Maricela had meant nothing to him, that she had been a companion to make him forget what had gone wrong with his marriage. Julia wanted to manipulate him, and he needed no one to do that for him. Now he could only discard their breakup as a mishap, a misunderstanding, or, as Pilar had said, "A lesson for him to learn from."

But he hadn't learned a thing—or, well, if anything, that being close to someone was better than being alone. Loneliness killed. Hurt. And it seemed, as he watched Pilar, that her loneliness stretched beyond the hurting stage.

7.

"You haven't forgotten, have you?" Armando said.

"What?" Pilar said, still watching the action on the screen.

On impulse, Armando stood and turned off the annoying noise.

"What did you do that for?"

"It's time we talk. Isn't that the reason why Julia left us alone?"

Pilar tried to stand, but Armando blocked her way. "Turn it back on!"

"Talk. Get everything that's bothering you out."

"You're crazy. I have nothing to say to you," she said. The mug trembled in her hand.

"What do you want from me?"

"Nothing. I need nothing."

"Then why do you ignore me?"

"I'm not ignoring you."

"You've never forgotten that day you saw me with Maricela at El Pueblo?"

"Ask Julia if she's forgotten. I don't care."

"You didn't care that I was with another woman?"

"What I care about's that you left Julia. You got bored with her, didn't you? Then you returned, and look what has happened. I hope I don't have to raise your child. If you don't love my daughter, why did you marry her?" She stood up, pushed Armando out of her way, and turned the T.V. back on.

"It's not that I don't love her ... "

"If you don't, why did you come back? To torment her? To make her suffer more?"

"Your daughter was an impossible person to live with," he said, trying to keep his voice down. "She wanted to run my life."

"Have you ever asked how she felt about you? I think you left her, and now you're back to ruin her."

"Christ, that's not true!"

"Don't curse in this house!" Pilar shouted.

"You're not being fair."

"Armando, please, let me watch. I told you, I don't have anything against you, except when it concerns my daughter."

"Maricela meant nothing to me."

"But does Julia know that? Have you told her?"

"I thought you did?"

"Never a word. All along I've tried to stay out of my daughter's marriage."

8.

Armando left the living room and went to the kitchen to cool off. His throat felt scratchy. He drank a cold glass of water, then returned. Pilar's words still echoed in his mind.

"How's Gustavo? Have you heard from him?" he asked.

"I don't want to talk about that bastard," she said, her lips unsticking from the mug slowly.

9.

At their wedding, Armando had been close enough to smell the Cuba Libres in Gustavo's breath. It was during the reception (Julia and Armando had already sliced the cake and were getting ready to depart for their honeymoon) that Gustavo approached Armando. At first, Gustavo fumbled with his words as though he was deeply moved by the sight of Julia dressed in white. He began by saying that Julita was his treasure, to take care of her, and to love her ... Then he said, "I'm not one for sayings, but ... " He paused to suck the last drops of rum from the ice cubes in the plastic cup. "A woman ... you want to know the truth, Armandito? I can't stand the sight of my wife in the morning. And she probably can't stand me, but she pretends better that I do. Her body's a constant reminder that I'm getting old, that I'm going to die ... But a woman, a woman's that darkness that prevents a man from finding the light switch. What a mystery they are." The other time he had met Gustavo, it was at the bank, during a long wait at the teller window. He revealed his plans to leave for Miami, then mentioned something about buying an apartment complex in Puerto Rico.

10.

Pilar glanced at Armando. "Did Julia tell you we're looking for a house?" he said.

"No, she hasn't. She's been so busy with her first graders."

"Now with the baby we're going to need more room," he said.

"Do you have the money?"

"Little, with what I've managed to save from the construction work. But Julia was thinking of asking—"

"Tell her to get the idea out of her mind. Her father'd never lend her the money."

11.

The pictures on the wall hung loosely on their wires—all pictures of Julia's evolution from diapers to ruffles to graduation cap and gown to the silk dress and veil.

"The two of you need a new beginning," Pilar said. "If only I'd have known, I would have never come here. Look what has happened to my family. What am I going to do here all by myself? You know I have nothing against this country, but ... Nonsense. Has Julia come up with a name yet?"

"No, we haven't."

"One'll come."

She ran the tip of her finger around the brim of the cup.

"Pilar, why do people change?"

She took a moment as though the question puzzled her, then answered, "If I knew, all my problems would be solved."

"I was in a bind," Armando said. "Our romance vanished in the blink of our eyes. We lost our desire for each other."

"So you thought by leaving her all your problems would be solved? You should never take shortcuts, Armando. They don't lead anywhere."

"I knew that if I didn't get away things would get worse."

"And you decided to run to another woman?"

"That just happened!"

"Just happened," Pilar repeated, then swallowed the last of her coffee.

12.

She stood up and went to the kitchen. Armando heard her open the faucet and wash her mug. "He ran away," she said. "He ran away to another woman."

Watching Pilar slouch back onto the divan made Armando feel sorry for her. "He'll be back and like a fool I'll take him back."

Armando was tired of quarrels. His eyes burned as if the heater had been shoved close to his face.

"You're all the same ... And you watch, he'll be back to have me—"

"Don't. Don't do it. You don't have to take him back."

Gustavo, Armando thought, might never return; he had no reason to.

"She did," Pilar said, looking up at the pictures.

"I'm not Gustavo," he said.

"I'll take him back. I always do." She wiped the saggy skin under her eyes with the tips of her fingers. "But I'll never forgive him."

"Just like you won't forgive me," he said.

"You're her problem." She stared at him the way she had looked at Maricela that hot August afternoon, the way a snake sizes up its rat, and he knew that at that moment she was blaming him for her life.

13.

A car drove up the driveway. The motor choked to a stop. The door slammed shut. Quick footsteps approached the front door, while fingers tried to get ahold of the right key. The door opened and then, Julia.

Pilar pushed herself up from the divan and walked toward her daughter as if to hug her.

Julia walked in from the cold, holding a large, grease-stained box with her mittens still on. Mother and daughter exchanged glances. Julia dropped her keys on the coffee table—a careless act Armando always hated—and walked into the kitchen.

"What took you so long?" he said, following her.

"I went shopping first," Julia said, putting the box down on the table and removing her mittens. "Mother," she shouted, her voice echoing among the dirty dishes, dripping faucet, grease-spattered stove and strewn newspapers, "would you like a slice?"

"Not hungry," Pilar shouted back.

She didn't want to sit with him, he thought, and be reminded of her misery.

"What did you say to her?" Julia said.

"Tried to settle our differences, that's all."

"Why's my mother upset?"

"Because of your father. Julia, please, let's eat."

Julia cut the largest slice. The cheese stretched in long strings until they snapped and recoiled. He moved his hand over to touch Julia's as she served him a slice. It felt clammy, cheese-greasy smooth. "I don't want to argue any more."

"What's that all about?" she asked.

He shrugged his shoulders. Here from the kitchen, he thought he heard soft weeping noises rising over the T.V.

"Mother?" Julia said, standing up and walking out of the kitchen.

Alone now, he reached for the knife and separated another slice, putting it onto his plate. He had promised so many things. So many things. To love and to honor ... He chewed his piece of crust as though it were his penance, as he told himself over and over like a litany, that a good father never abandoned his child.

A Perfect Hotspot

THIS idea of selling ice cream during the summer seems ridiculous, pointless. I'd much rather be close to water. The waves. Where I can hear them tumble in and then roll out, and see the tiny bubbles left behind on the sand pop one by one. Or feel the undercurrents warm this time of year. Swimming. Watching the girls in bikinis with sand stuck to the backs of their thighs walk up and down the boardwalk. At this time of the morning, the surfers are out riding the waves.

Instead I'm inside an ice cream truck with my father, selling, cruising the streets. The pumps suck oil out of the ground rapidly with the creaking sounds of iron biting iron in a fenced lot at the end of the street. They look like giant rocking horses. Father turns at the corner, then, suddenly, he points to another ice cream truck.

"There's the competition," he says. "If the economy doesn't improve soon, these streets'll be full of them."

He's smoking, and the smoke floats back my way and chokes me. I can't stand it. Some of the guys on the swim team smoke. I don't understand how they can smoke and do their best when it's time for competition. I wouldn't smoke. To do so would be like cheating myself out of winning.

All morning he's been instructing me on how to sell ice cream.

"Tonio," he says now, "come empty your pockets."

I walk to the front of the truck, stick my hands deep into my pockets and grab a handful of coins—what we've made in change all morning. The coins fall, overlap and multiply against the sides of the grease-smudged, change box. I turn my pockets inside-out until the last coin falls. He picks out the pieces of lint and paper from the coins.

When he begins to explain the truck's quirks, "the little problems," as he calls the water leaks, burning oil, and dirty carburetor, I return to the back of the truck and sit down on top of the wood counter next to the window.

"Be always on the lookout for babies," father says. "The ones in pampers. They pop out of nowhere. Check your mirrors all the time."

A CAUTION CHILDREN cardboard sign hangs from the rearview mirror. Running over children is a deep fear that seems to haunt him.

All I need, I keep reminding myself, is to pass the CPR course, get certified, and look for a job as a beach lifeguard.

"Stop!" a kid screams, slamming the screen door of his house open. He runs to the grassy part next to the sidewalk. Father stops the truck. The kid's hand comes up over the edge of the window with a dollar bill forked between his little fingers.

"What do you want?" I say.

"A Froze Toe," he says, jumping up and down, dirt rings visible on his neck. He wets the corners of his mouth with his cherry, Kool-aid-stained tongue. I reach inside the freezer and bring out a bar. On its wrapper is the picture of an orange foot with a blue bubble gum ball on the big toe.

"See what else he wants," father says. "Make sure they always leave the dollar."

The kid takes his ice cream, and he smiles.

"What else?" I ask him.

He shrugs his shoulders, shakes his head, and bites the wrapper off. The piece of paper falls on the grass. I give him his change; he walks back to his house.

"Should always make sure they leave all the money they bring," father says. "They get it to spend it. That's the only way you'll make a profit. Don't steal their money, but exchange it for merchandise." His ears stick out from underneath his L.A. Dodgers cap. The short hair on the back of his head stands out.

I grin up at the rearview mirror, but he isn't looking.

"Want to split a Pepsi, Tonio?" he says.

"I'm not thirsty."

"Get me some water then."

The cold mist inside the freezer crawls up my hand. After he drinks and returns the bottle, I place it back with the ice cream.

"Close the freezer," he says, "before all the cold gets out and they melt."

If the cold were out I'd be at the natatorium doing laps.

○ ○ ○

On another street, a group of kids jumps and skips around a short man. The smallest of the kids hangs from the man's thigh. The man signals my father to stop, then walks up to the window. The kids scream excitedly.

"Want this one, daddy," one of the girls says.

"This one!" a boy says.

The smallest kid jumps, pointing his finger at the display my father has made with all the toys and candies.

"No, Jose," the man says, taking the kid by the wrist. "No candy."

The kid turns to look up at his father, not fully understanding, and then looks at me. His little lips tremble.

"Give me six Popsicles," the man says.

"I don't want no Pop—"

"Popsicles or nothing. I don't have money to buy you what you want."

"A Blue Ghost. I want a Blue Ghost."

"No, I said."

The smallest kid cries.

"Be quiet, Jose, or I'm going to tell the man to go away."

I put the six Popsicles on the counter.

"How much?" the man asks. The skin around his eyes is a darker brown than that of his nose and cheeks.

"A dollar-fifty," I say.

He digs inside his pockets and produces two wrinkled green balls which he throws on the counter. The two dollar bills roll. I unfold the bills, smooth them, and give them to father, who returns the man his change through the front window.

The man gives each kid a Popsicle, then walks away with his hands in his pockets. Jose, still crying, grabs his as he follows his father back to their house.

"He doesn't want to spend his beer money," father says, driving away from the curb.

After that, we have no more customers for hours. Ever since he brought the truck home two years ago, father has changed. Ice creams have become his world. According to father, appearance and cleanliness isn't important as long as the truck passes the Health Department inspection in order to obtain the sales license. The inside of the truck is a mess: paint flakes off, rust hides between crevices, the freezer lids hold layer upon layer of dirt and melted ice cream. Here I'll have to spend the rest of my summer, I think, among the strewn Doritos, Munchos, and the rest of the merchandise.

The outside of the truck had been painted by father's friend, Gaspar, before mother died. I remember how Gaspar drank beer after beer while he painted the crown over the K in KING OF ICE CREAM and assured mother, who never missed one of my swim meets and who always encouraged me to become the best swimmer I could be, that I was going to make it all right in the end.

Father lives this way, I know, out of loneliness. He misses mother as much as I do.

I count the passing of time by how many ice creams I sell. It isn't anything like swimming laps. Doing laps involves the idea of setting and breaking new limits.

"How much do you think we have?" my father asks. The visor of his cap tilts upward.

"I don't know." I hate the metallic smell money leaves on my fingers.

"Any idea?"

"No."

"A couple of months on your own and you'll be able to guess approximately how much you make."

A couple of months, I think, and I'll be back in high school. Captain of the varsity swim team. A customer waits down the street.

"Make the kill fast," father says.

A barefooted woman holding a child to her breast comes to the window. She has dirty fingernails, short and uneven, as if she bites them all the time. Make the kill fast, I think.

Ice creams on the counter, I tell her, "Two dollars."

She removes the money out of her brassiere and hands it to me, then she walks away. She has yellow blisters on the back of each heel.

After that, he begins to tell me the story of the wild dog. When he was a kid, a wild bitch came down from the hills and started killing my grandfather's chickens. "Seeing the scattered feathers," father says, "made your grandfather so angry I thought his face would burst because it'd turned so red."

"Anyway," he continues, "the wild dog kept on killing chickens."

Not only my grandfather's, but other farmers' as well. The other farmers were scared because they thought the wild dog was a witch. One morning, my grandfather got my father out of bed early and took him up to the hills behind the house with a jar of poison. A farmer had found the bitch's litter. My grandfather left my father in charge of anointing the poison all over the puppies fur so that when the mother came back, if he hadn't shot it by then, she'd die the minute she licked her young. My father didn't want to do it, but my grandfather left him in command while he went after the wild dog to shoot it. The dog disappeared and the puppies licked each other to death.

When he finishes telling me the story, father looks at the rearview mirror and grins, then he drives on. He turns up the volume in the music box and now *Raindrops Keep Falling On My Head* blares out of the speakers. The old people'll complain, he says, because the loud music hurts their eardrums, but the louder the music, the more people'll hear it, and more ice creams'll get sold.

Farther ahead, another kid stops us. The kid has his tongue out. His eyes seem to be too small for his big face. Though he seems old, he still drools. He claps his small hands quickly.

"Does he have money?" father asks.

"Can't see."

The kid walks over to the truck and hangs from the edge of the window.

"Get him away from the truck," father says, then to the kid, "Hey, move away!"

"Come on," I tell the kid, "you might fall and hurt yourself."

"Wan icleam," the kid says.

"We'll be back in a little while," father tells him.

"Wan icleam!" He doesn't let go. "Wan icleam!"

"Move back!" father shouts. "Tonio, get him away from the truck."

I try to unstick the kid's pudgy fingers from the metal edge of the window, but he won't let go. His saliva falls on my hands.

"Wan icleam!"

I reach over to one of the shelves to get a penny candy for him so that I can bait him into letting go, but father catches me.

"Don't you dare," he says.

He opens the door and comes around the back to the kid, pulling him away from the truck to the sidewalk where he sets the kid down, and returns.

"Can't give your merchandise away," he says. "You can't make a profit that way, Tonio."

The kid runs after us shouting, waving his arms. I grab a handful of candies and throw them out the window to the sidewalk, where they fall on the grass and scatter.

∘　∘　∘

The sun sets slowly, and, descending, it spreads Popsicle orange on the sky. Darkness creeps on the other side of the city.

If I don't get a job as a lifeguard, I think, then I'm going to travel southeast and visit the islands.

"How are the ice creams doing?" father asks. "Are they softening?"

I check by squeezing a bar and say, "I think we should call it a day."

"Tonio," he says. He turns off the music, makes a left turn to the main street, and heads home. "Why didn't you help me with that kid? You could have moved him. What will happen when you're here by yourself?"

"Couldn't do it."

"Here," he says, giving me the change box. "Take it inside when we get home."

"I'll get it when we get there."

He puts the blue box back down on top of the stand he built over the motor. Cars speed by. The air smells heavy with exhaust and chemical fumes. In the distance, columns of smoke rise from factory smokestacks.

He turns into the driveway, drives the truck all the way to the front of the garage, and parks underneath the long branches of the avocado tree.

"Take the box inside," he says, turning off the motor. He steps down from the truck and connects the freezer to the extension cord coming out of the kitchen window.

I want to tell him that I won't come out tomorrow.

"Come on, Tonio. Bring the box in."

"You do it," I say.

"What's the matter, son?"

"I'd rather you do it."

"Like you'd rather throw all my merchandise out of the window," he says, growing red in the face. "I saw you."

He walks toward me, and I sense another argument coming. Father stops in front of me and gives me a wry smile. "Dreamers like you," he says, "learn the hard way."

He turns around, picks up the change box, and says, "I'm putting the truck up for sale. From now on you're on your own, you hear. I'm not forcing you to do something you don't want to."

I don't like the expressionless look on his face when usually, whenever he got angry at me, his face would get red and sweaty.

He unlocks the kitchen door and enters the house.

I jump out of the truck, lock the door, and walk around our clapboard house to the patio. Any moment now, I think, father'll start slamming doors inside and throwing things around. He'll curse. I lean against the wall and feel the glass of the window behind me when it starts to tremble.

Full House

THE room Danny enters used to be his brother's but there are men in it now who play poker, talk too loud, and chainsmoke. Cigar smoke chokes Danny.

"Serve them first," his father demands, not looking up from his cards.

"Hey, *Ratón*," Coco, one of the men whom Danny's brother, Big Rudy, nicknamed The Ghost because he's so white and pale, says to Danny, "haven't seen you around." *Ratón* means mouse. "What's the matter? Don't you like us any more?"

"The only rat here's you," Danny says, placing a plate of steaming rice, fried plantains and fricaseed porkchops in front of him.

"Respect," his father says.

Coco's got a pair of tens, a five, and two more cards facing the green felt. He laughs and puffs smoke at Danny.

Rigo, Danny's father, keeps the cards fanned between his hands. As Danny walks behind him, he can see the pair of twos, the Jack of Clubs, a six, and the Queen of Spades in his clay-colored hands. Rigo runs his fingers through his curly hair, which daily seems to be getting lighter and lighter, like cigarette ash. "Come baby, come," he says, licking his lips.

"Cut the shit," Coco says, biting down on his cigar, smoke clouding his narrow, beady eyes.

These same faces have been coming and going for as long as Danny can remember—since Big Rudy took off and left the house—except for the man now sitting between Coco and Quezada, who everybody calls Jaws because of his big mouth. The man looks like an old cowboy, skin taut over cheekbones and jaw, except for the wrinkles around the eyes. His eyes have a yellowish gleam which makes Danny nervous to even try and peek at the man's cards.

"The girl makes me nervous," the man says, looking at Adela, Danny's sister, who's been sitting in the corner, but not far enough from the table to be unnoticed.

"Adelita?" Quezada says.

"Leave my girl alone," Coco tells the man, "and play." He stares at Adela, who turns to look out the window at the passing cars. She sits on the windowsill in tight white shorts, her legs baby talcum powder smooth and tanned. This isn't the same sister he used to take to the corner market for pop and candies before Rudy left. Adela, who often woke Danny in the middle of the night because her tummy hurt or she was having a bad dream.

Danny finishes serving the food, then works his way around it again removing the soggy napkins and empty glasses in which cigar butts float. The stranger paws greedily at his food with dirty fingers.

"Watch my cigar," he says to Danny, moving the ashtray out of the way.

Danny approaches his sister and says to her in his tired, whispery voice, "Mother wants to see you".

"Father needs me here," she says.

"Helping him cheat?"

"Quiet," she says, knitting her eyebrows, "don't say that. You know Coco and Quezada understand."

"Well, you are."

She looks away and he sees the back of her earring, a

tiny golden bow pinching her skin.

"Mother wants you downstairs."

"Get out of here."

"Now!"

"Tell her to wait," she says.

His mother has waited long enough. He hurries past the stranger. From the door he looks back and catches Adela giving their father signals.

Ever since Adela's grown up, all she does is side with father, he thinks, especially now that he's going through a streak of bad luck. Sometimes it seems she likes Rigo better than her mother, but perhaps it's only because mother's always telling her what to do.

Danny can't stand living in the house any more. Too much going on for him to keep track of, and now that he's in high school there's no reason why he should be serving all these men who come to gamble. Let them order their food from a restaurant and have it delivered. But he does it for the tips these men give him.

It's been almost a year since Rudy fought with father and got thrown out of the house. That day after the fight, Danny recalls, Rudy packed a suitcase and said he was going to Miami. He didn't even say goodbye, but later he wrote Danny to tell him that he made it out there all right and got a job at a gas station. Soon he'd send enough money for Danny to pay for the trip.

Downstairs, Danny finds his mother, who's been laid off from the cannery, bent against the formica countertop in the kitchen, her face buried in the crook of her elbow. He stands on the other side of the counter close to the boxes of Twix and Fruit Loops cereal and the plastic cast miniatures of his mother's favorite saints in front of which a candle burns. He asks her what's wrong.

She doesn't say anything. Behind her on the wall there's a high school portrait of Rudy. His brother has a sneaky smile as though the photographer taking the picture had told him a dirty joke. Rudy's rope-blonde hair is neatly combed to the side.

His mother straightens up and stirs the white rice in one casserole, then removes another filled with chunks of meat from the red-hot grill. "Don't let any of those men get close to your sister," she says.

"I told her you wanted to see her, but she won't come down."

She wears the cuffs of her pants rolled. Some of the straps on her jellybean sandals are torn. These are the same clothes she's been wearing for so long to work, to bed, to go grocery shopping. Her moppy-looking hair hasn't been touched in weeks. He wishes she'd stop smoking.

The real reason Rudy left, Danny thinks, is that mother stands behind father in whatever father decides to do. Adela takes after her. Perhaps mother hasn't forgiven Rudy for punching father in the mouth, for knocking out his front teeth which cost mother a whole month's paycheck.

Almost noon and the sky's still gray and sunless. If his brother were here, Danny thinks, they'd be at the park playing catch or throwing a football. Anything's better than running food upstairs.

"What's Adela doing?" she asks.

"She's watching the game."

"I hope they plan to end soon."

"Doubt it."

She spoons equal amounts of food on to three more plates. How does she do it? he thinks. How does she juggle all the things that she does at the same time: cooking, dishes, laundry, cleaning?

Danny's mother places the plates on his hands carefully. They are hot, and the heat tickles the palms of his hands and forearms. The fear that he might drop the plates on his way up the stairs produces a sweat, a film of it on his forehead and cheeks.

"Get your sister away from that room," she says.

"I wish they'd choke."

As Danny starts up the stairs, Adela comes running out of the room. "Don't go up," she says out of breath.

"What's going on?" asks Danny.

"That new man's arguing with father. Caught him cheating. The man says he wants his money back."

See, Danny wants to say, didn't I tell you. Cheating leads to trouble, Big Rudy ... Something slams against the wall. Chips fall on the floor.

"Come to the kitchen," Adela says.

Danny follows her to the kitchen and puts the plates down. His mind races through a long list of things his brother would do. For example, Rudy'd run upstairs and find out what's really happening. Rudy's not chicken like he is, Danny thinks.

Every thump makes the lamp hanging over the dining room table tremble. There is a moment of silence during which his mother stands still, looking up at the ceiling, then at her miniature saints.

Someone slams a door upstairs, then hurries down the stairs. The man shouts, "I'm coming back!" He leaves the front door wide open.

"Mother," Adela says, "I didn't mean to—"

"Go to the patio. Both of you," Danny's mother says.

"See," Danny says, "that's what you get for cheating."

Danny expects his mother to know what to do; she's lived through all this longer than he intends to. His mother disappears up the stairs.

Adela leads the way outside. She sits against the stucco wall by the side of the house.

"You think he'll really do it?" she asks. "Come back."

Danny shrugs.

She picks at a scab on her elbow.

"You should've seen him," she says. "His face so red, God. Then he threw a handful of chips at father's face."

"How did the man catch you?"

"Saw father signaling," she says, looking at the wrinkled skin on her elbow. "Then he started picking up things and throwing them all over the place. A chair almost hit Quezada on the head."

"Sometimes I wish dad would get the hell out of this house," Danny says.

"Mother'd be lonely."

"Remember the fight with Rudy. I thought Rudy was going to kick his ass out."

"I remember."

Father lost about three thousand dollars that afternoon and he took it out on Rudy.

"Mother's told you not to go upstairs," Danny tells his sister.

"What do you want me to do? Say no to him. Say, 'Go to hell, dad'."

Her features sink on her face and make her look sad. Her lips quiver.

"Can't play like he used to," she says.

"He should stop gambling and get a job like mother's told him to."

Danny's parents argue upstairs, his father shouting to be left alone, that he's had enough persecution in the old country.

Is Rigo the same person who sat him on his lap and told him cockfight stories? Danny thinks. His father'd promised to stop playing poker.

"Stand by your man, so the song goes," Adela says.

"Crap," Danny says. "Don't you let this happen to you."

"You'd never leave like Rudy did, would you?" Adela rests her head against the wall and closes her eyes.

"I don't know," he says. "I want to."

"Rudy's a coward."

"Bullshit," Danny says.

"It's the truth."

"You never saw," Danny says and stops to tear a handful of grass out of the lawn.

"What didn't I see?"

"The way Rudy hit father. I thought he was going to kill him."

"And you didn't do anything?"

"What could I do?"

"Stop them."

"I stood there wanting Rudy to go on. That's the truth."

"Think about this," she says softly. "Maybe it isn't his fault, but mother's. She married him. It was her choice. If she really wanted dad to leave, she wouldn't sleep with him."

"What are you saying?"

"Father's not as bad as you make him sound. Besides, he's *our* father. Don't complain." Adela stands and moves toward the fence away from Danny.

"All I want's for him to stop gambling, that's all."

Coco and Quezada chatter on their way out of the house. They climb into Coco's car and drive away. "Those bastards," Danny says.

It's now the time of the afternoon when the sky ceases to be gray. There is only the buzz of the refrigerator to disturb the silence in the kitchen.

Danny follows his sister inside. Adela sits on the sofa and listens to the radio. He thinks of Rudy and what he must be doing right now.

A car drives up the driveway and stops suddenly.

"He's here," Adela says, jumping up from the sofa. She runs upstairs.

"Stay here!" Danny shouts to her, but it's too late.

Climbing over the patio fence into the vacant lot, he thinks that he doesn't want to stick around to see what might happen. He runs around the corner to the front of the house. The thought of the man hurting his mother and sister makes him want to interfere, but he knows better.

The man enters the house. There's a shot, its report echoes between the walls of the neighboring apartment building and his.

"Rigo stay inside!" Danny's mother says from upstairs.

Danny enters the living room and runs up the stairs to find the man trying to kick the door open. "Open up, you son-of-a-bitch!"

Big Rudy, Danny thinks, might have easily stood in the man's way.

The door slams open.

"Hide, Adela. Stay out of the way!" Danny's mother says. She stands against the wall at the other end of the hall. "Rigo, don't let my daughter get hurt!"

Danny runs up from behind and jumps on the man's back.

Too late. The gun goes off and the bullet hits Rigo's shoulder. The man drops the gun. Rigo groans as he covers the red spot. Adela picks up the money and throws it at the man who tries to reach for the revolver on the floor.

Danny holds onto both the man's legs, but the man frees one and kicks Danny in the nose. Danny feels the warmth of his blood trickling into his mouth. It tastes salty like sweat. Another kick, this one to his head, and he lets go.

The man collects his money, and when he's about to reach for his revolver, Adela picks it up and throws it out the window. The man pushes her and she trips over the upturned table.

Danny tries to get up as the man runs past him on the way out.

While Rigo lies unconscious on the floor, Danny's mother calls the police. Fighting nausea, Danny helps his sister up and they both go downstairs.

Big Rudy would have stopped the man, Danny thinks; then, that's it, tonight he leaves. He sits next to Adela and gives in to his drowsiness.

The police arrive followed by the ambulance. Danny translates what his mother tells the policemen. "Don't mention the gambling," his mother says. Adela joins him in the poker room. She's got her father's blood on her shorts.

One of the paramedics feels Rigo's ribs to see if they're broken, then he gives Danny a gauze pad to hold against his nose. Danny watches them lift his father onto the stretcher and carry him down to the ambulance. His mother helps the paramedics.

Adela walks to the living room window and stands there as motionless as a garden statue. His mother returns and says she's going to the hospital. "I'll call you from there," she says.

"Don't go to him," Danny tells her.

As his mother looks for her sweater in the vestibule closet, she asks all the saints not to let anything be wrong with her Rigo.

"Keep your head back," his mother tells him, then to Adela, "Are you all right, honey?"

"I'm fine, mother," she says. Then, when their mother leaves the house, Adela looks at Danny and shrugs.

Danny's dark blood stains the minute squares on the gauze while he sits on one of the kitchen chairs. Adela comes to him in the kitchen, opens the refrigerator, takes ice out of the freezer and wraps the cubes in mother's apron. "This'll stop the bleeding," she says.

"Does it look bad?" Danny asks, swallowing a gob of blood.

She says something, but he can't hear. His heart beats loudly between his ears.

"There," his sister says, her cold hands touching his forehead. "You can show-off now. You can say you beat the man up."

Danny closes his eyes and tries to remember what just took place.

Adela smiles down at Danny, who holds on to the ice which begins to burn against his bruise while blood leaks slowly down to his throat. The sound of the siren echoes inside the house and slowly begins to fade in the distance.

Settlements

BE IT KNOWN:

I. I stole shoes and cash out of the register from the department store where I worked as a shoe salesman.

II. On a Friday, a week before inventory, I quit, took a girl from Lingerie and spent the evening with her in my one bedroom apartment.

III. Later, after she left, I smoked a joint and called my mother to tell her I was leaving Los Angeles.

IV. My mother, the lawyer, blamed my father for my "aimlessness" in life (two years out of high school and I didn't want to go to college) and hung up.

The last time I saw my father was during lunch and he was drunk. I often wondered if the people who bought houses from him ever smelled the stink of alcohol on his breath. Between swigs (I drank beer; he cognac, straight up) I told him I was leaving L.A.

"Oh," he said, "why?"

"Got to get away," I said. "Can't stand the bumper-to-bumper course my life's taking. My painting's going nowhere."

"Your mother's got nothing to do with this, does she?" he asked, giving me one of his you're-full-of-shit stares from behind his thick-framed glasses. My father had divorced my mother five years ago.

"I want to prove to her that I'm headed in the right direction."

"What direction's that, son?"

"Southeast," I said. "I want to go to the desert. Fill up the gas tank and ride, ride, ride."

"That'll only get you to Blythe," he said and smiled.

"Blythe's desert, isn't it," I said.

"Coyote and Gila Monster territory," he said.

Later that same day, I packed my clothes, sleeping bag, portfolio and art supplies, got my last Michelob out of the fridge, jumped in my Mustang and split.

WHEREAS:

By morning I found myself in Tucson, Arizona. There I was. In Prickly Pear and Saguaro cactus country. Sand and pebbles as shiny as mother-of-pearl buttons. Rocks, boulders, mountains, canyons, strange looking lizards and rodents, such was the desert as I had never seen it.

On the way to the foothills, I stopped for lunch at a Denny's. I asked the waitress if she knew of any places for rent in the vicinity.

"Look in the university paper," she said.

For that much information I left her an Honest Abe neatly folded under the ashtray, paid my bill, and set out to seek some shelter.

Sure enough in the university paper I found this under ROOMMATES WANTED: Seeking responsible person to share a 3br 1bath house / walking distance / washer & dryer / $175permth half utilities.

The adobe house stood behind a couple of mesquite bushes and a fence far gone to rust. The house rested on a brick foundation. The name, B. TRISTE, was painted on the side of the mailbox. I opened the torn screen door and knocked. At first I heard nothing, then quick footsteps, and a young woman opened the door.

"The place still for rent?" I asked.

"Oh yeah," she said, "sure, come on in."

"Fuentes," I introduced myself, "Lucas Fuentes."

"Becky," she said.   She had mossy-green eyes and caramel skin. No bra, so the nipples bounced around and poked at the cloth of her flannel shirt. When she started to show me the place, I got a good look at her small ass.

"Stop," I said. We came to a halt in the hall. "Look at this face and tell me I don't look responsible?"

She flashed a you've-got-to-be-kidding smile. "Oh, you do," she said, "but please look at this place carefully. See if you like it first."

Becky showed me the rest of the house, pointing out what couldn't or would be fixed. Cracks on the bedroom walls. Stains on the ceiling. In the extra room (she used it as a study) paint had sealed the windows shut.

"Are you a student?" she asked in the bathroom. Her voice echoed among the broken tiles and faucet leak stains.

"Nope," I told her. "Left L.A. and came here to work on my painting."

"You're an artist?"

I asked her what she did for a living.

"Sing opera," she said as she led me back to the living room. "I'm a voice major at U of A. Getting my Masters in two more semesters."

I asked, "Opera?"

"I've played Musetta in *La Boheme.* Smaller part in

Cosi Fan Tute. Next semester I expect to get a leading role in *La Traviatta.*"

"Luciano Pavarotti's all I know about operas," I said.

"That's a start," she said. "He's good."

"I need a place," I told her and backed to the door.

She went over the money arrangements slowly. I wrote her a check for $350 (money from an account I opened with what I made from the shoe sales), part rent and part deposit, and slapped it into the palm of her white hand.

"I'm easy to live with," I told her.

"Guess I'll find out soon enough," she said.

I left her standing on the porch and I went out to get the stuff from my car, which was covered with dust and dead insects, and moved in.

WHEREAS:

Sunset after sunset I sat on the rotting porch steps and watched the sky blaze. In the desert the night came about quickly, bringing with it the noises of cicadas and crickets and of the wind sifting through the dry foliage. From inside the house, the sounds of Becky playing her flute, long, pipey whistles, rang in my ears. When it wasn't the flute, then it was her singing. She practiced by warming up fortissimo and mellowing down to a steady, hum-like bass.

Usually I sat there and felt happy that I was getting a lot of work done, for something wonderful began to happen to my work. Each canvas that I stretched, gessoed and added texture to came alive. Sepia, burnt sienna, raw umber, rust, and some of the lighter earth colors snuck on to my palette. The paintings began to look like ancient treasure maps. Blue-prints to old civilizations was what they really looked like, full of broken lines and shapes and things I cut up and glued on. Sometimes I took a spatula and smeared lots of paint on huge areas or I threw a handful of sand at the finished painting to give it a gritty texture.

I worked all afternoons until Becky returned from her part-time job at a fast food restaurant, then I'd come out to talk to her.

During those first couple of weeks, I got to know her well. Sometimes she put on a classical record (Bach, Mozart, Beethoven, et al.) and walked out of the house and joined me on the porch.

"Missed it," I said. "A hawk landed on that mesquite. It had a frog hanging from its beak. It just—" I snapped my fingers—"flew away the instant you walked out."

She told me that when she graduated she was going to go to Miami to take lessons from a voice coach and teach to support herself.

I mentioned as little as possible about my life, about my parents and how their divorce changed my life because I no longer felt connected to anything. At one time their marriage was my foundation. As soon as my father moved out of the house and my mother drafted the divorce settlement and they both signed it, I didn't care anymore what I did or where I went.

One evening, Becky brought out a miniature calumet and we smoked grass. She kept asking me what I was going to do for money.

"Work," I said. "But I haven't run out yet, so why worry?"

"I like you," she said. "When I first saw you I knew you were going to be easygoing."

I asked her to close her eyes and try to describe what she thought I looked like.

"Umm," she said, "can see your eyes. The way wrinkles form on the edges there." She touched the corner of my eye with her finger. "Chicken-scratch like. Let's see. Color? Color?" She opened her eyes and looked at me.

"Black," I said, "habit black. I hate them."

She grew quiet for a while then told me that for the longest time she had wanted to move away from home, and now she was content to be out on her own.

WHEREAS:

Jogging one night, I raced her back to the house and she beat me because I fell and scraped the upper side of my right leg. A bad slide. Anyway, the bruise burned and itched like crazy. She helped me up into the house, sat me on the sofa, left the living room, and returned with a first-aid kit.

"This is going to hurt," she said and pulled my shorts down.

Pain shot up my leg and I twisted and turned, my hands folded into tight fists, but I took the pain while she cleaned the scrape, then cotton-swabbed it with iodine.

Her face drew too close to mine. I grabbed her by the hood of her sweatshirt and kissed her. "I couldn't take it any more, you know," I said.

She took me by the hand and helped me get to her bed. She helped me undress.

"Go slow," I said.

"This," she said, climbing into bed, "heals all. Cures all."

WHEREAS:

October 16, 19—

Dear Mother:
Made it out to Tucson okay, and plan to stay. Nobody's fault, you understand? I'm happy. You're happy. He's happy. Happy, the all-American adjective. Say hello to Mr. Century 21, the real realtor himself. Just in case you're wondering what I'm up to, I've met an American girl, diva-to-be opera singer. Anyway, love's brewing. Take care.

Still Cultured,

Rattlesnake

WHEREAS:

ESPERANZA L. MURILLO

October 29, 19—

Dear Son:
Ever since you left, I've been praying to Saint Jude. Know who that is? Patron saint of hopeless cases. I've heard via one of the girls who called to find out where you were what you did at the store. So that's how you managed to support yourself, eh? Your father doesn't know. Here's a check for five hundred, half mine, half his. We both took a guess at your present living conditions. Chasing women still? Now it's an American Tweetybird. Who will it be tomorrow?

Love,

Misunderstood Mother

WHEREAS:

We wasted no time planning camping trips. Three in a row, since Becky didn't work on the weekends and wasn't rehearsing for any opera parts.

Weekend #1: To Sabino Canyon, not too far from where we lived. Nice place with a ravine banked with beds of purple and yellow, wild flowers and fishhook cacti. We played see-who-spots-the-most-animals games.

She saw deer, roadrunners, an owl, a couple of hares and a fox. I found some kind of lizard sunbathing on top of a rock and asked Becky what it was.

"Gila monster," she said. "Come to Illinois with me for Christmas?"

"What's there?"

"I want you to meet my parents."

"Let me think about it," I said, then asked her what she thought of the saguaros.

"See how they stand?" she said, "With their arms bent up like that? It looks like they're saying, 'Don't shoot! Don't shoot!'"

Weekend #2: It was colder at the top of Mount Lemon when we finally drove up. We set up camp in the middle of a circle of pine trees, started a fire, and cooked hamburgers. In the night, after we made love she told me how much she really wanted me to visit Illinois.

"We can go Greyhound," she said, "that way you won't have to drive."

"In my book that's still two whole days on the road," I said, watching how the shadows moved on the canvas tent.

"C'mon, you'll love Illinois," she said. "I can take you down to Edwardsville. There are lots of old, rundown barns you can sketch. We can visit St. Louis. The zoo.

The arch."

"I'll think about it," I said.

She rolled over, away from me, and fell asleep.

Weekend #3: The trip to the Grand Canyon took longer, but, after a stopover at Flagstaff for lunch, we got there. All the campgrounds were full this time of year. No reservations, no stay. That night we had to sleep in the car, then spent all of the next day and part of Sunday going down and then back up a narrow trail. Becky seemed pensive and withdrawn.

Mules passed us on the way, snorting and wagging their tails. They made the air reek of piss. We had to keep looking down at the ground to make sure we didn't step on mule shit.

"How long would we stay?" I said.

She looked up at me (on the way up she was walking behind me, sometimes holding on to my belt) and said, "Where?"

"At your parents'," I said.

"Three or four days," she said, "no more than that, okay?"

"Go Greyhound," I sang, "and leave the driving to us!"

This made her so happy that when we got to the top she took me to a gift shop and bought me a cowboy hat with a leather band around it on which she pinned an I CLIMBED THE GRAND CANYON button.

I wasn't too excited because I felt that to meet her parents would be letting things get more serious than they should be at this stage in our relationship, but I gave in just to please her. That night, she let me sketch her in the nude, and we drank two bottles of wine and got drunk.

WHEREAS:

The trip. I found myself sitting next to Becky on the front seat of the bus behind the driver who, from Tucson to El Paso, chewed tobacco and spat into a styrofoam cup.

There was also this old woman sitting behind us who repeated, "I will take my cars and clothes and take them to the Salvation Army. He'll see." This became a litany. She chain-smoked, so the driver had to tell her to go to the back of the bus. Probably some woman who was getting divorced, I thought. It seemed like everybody in the world was getting divorced, so why get married?

Shortly before we arrived at the station in El Paso where we were supposed to change buses, the woman returned, sat behind us, then reached over and tapped me on the shoulder.

"Do you read the bible?" she said. "The Psalms?"

"Read them all," I told the woman, and this made Becky laugh so hard she had to hide her face. The woman left us alone after that.

WHEREAS:

Her parents were waiting for us at the station in Peoria. I couldn't guess who they were in the crowd of people there until this couple approached Becky from behind. I stood back while they took turns hugging and kissing their daughter.

Her father was a tall, white-haired, broad-shouldered man. He shook my hand and looked me over. I didn't like the red and blue veins on the tip of his nose.

I took Mrs. Triste's mittened hand and shook it with both of mine. She didn't let go right away. Instead, she held them and told me how utterly wonderful it was to make my acquaintance.

She had a small, round face, yellowish hair hidden under the hood of her coat, pudgy nose, lips the color of frozen meat.

"Happy to meet you," I said.

Snow covered the ground up to my ankles outside the bus station.

Her mother told us to get inside the car, that we were going to a restaurant for dinner. Feeling tired, dirty from the two days without a shower, I sat in the back of the Buick Regal and closed my eyes.

We arrived at the restaurant and Mrs. Triste was still talking about John Deere shutting down their plant. "A lot of people are leaving Peoria," she said, "and a lot of them come to Fred for counseling.

Becky's father was a marriage counselor, Ph.D in psychology. And her mother taught at a school for the mentally handicapped.

The conversation continued over dinner; I quickly ate my sirloin steak and mashed potatoes. Mr. Triste wasn't saying much. Mrs. Triste asked me where my parents lived.

"They're divorced," I said.

An opera buff just like his daughter, Mr. Triste started talking about what a terrible fate young Italian boys who were sopranos had in the 18th century. "Castrati sopranos," he said.

"Castrated sopranos?" I said. Mrs. Triste and Becky smiled, but Mr. Triste grew serious.

He didn't like me, I thought, because he probably figured I wasn't good enough for his daughter.

Dinner over, we drove to the house, a two-story, four bedroom place. They had bought it cheap, and were planning to restore and remodel most of it by next summer. I was glad to be getting out of the cold.

Mrs. Triste made hot chocolate and served it on the dining room table under which the wooden, waxed floors shone. Mr. Triste grew tired and said he was turning in.

"Make yourself at home here," Mrs. Triste said to me before she left, then to Becky, "Becky, show him to his room downstairs. Get a fire going in the fireplace if he wants. If not, get the portable heater out of the closet."

"I'll take care of him, mother," Becky said.

Her mother said goodnight and left.

"I want to go to sleep," I said.

"Party pooper."

Becky led me downstairs to what was to be my bedroom, started a fire in the fireplace, placed the screen in front of the flames, and fixed my bed.

"He doesn't like me," I said.

"Who? My father?"

"Did you see the way he kept looking at me?"

"You're crazy," she said, kissed me goodbye and left.

WHEREAS:

After dinner the following night, Mr. Triste asked me to accompany him outside to get more wood for the fireplace.

The cold snuck in through the cuffs of my Levi's and made me shudder as I followed Mr. Triste to the woodpile. There he brushed the snow off, picked up a couple of logs, and handed them to me.

"Never been in this kind of weather, eh?" he asked.

"I prefer warmth," I said.

"We want Becky to return here after she graduates," he said, putting three more logs on my arms.

"She plans to go to Miami and take voice lessons," I said.

"And you plan to follow her?"

I told him I didn't know.

"Well, you should know," he said, and picked out some logs for himself to carry. "Both of you must realize that it's going to be hard."

I asked him what he meant by "hard".

"You come from a different world than she does," he said, "and you're bound to have disagreements. Lots of them."

This made me angry, so I told him, "Becky's a big girl now, Mr. Triste. I think she knows what's good for her."

He walked back to the house in silence. Inside, he stacked the wood by the fireplace, washed his hands in the kitchen, and went to his room.

WHEREAS:

At 11:42 a.m. Becky woke me up. "Hey, sleepyhead," she said and kissed me. "I have a surprise for you." She walked over to the stereo. "We have the house all to ourselves," she said, searching through the records. She found the one she was looking for and put it on the turntable.

Becky removed her terry cloth robe and dropped it on the rug. "Listen," she said, climbing onto the bed, "and make love to me."

Wagner's *Ride of the Valkyries* started. It was loud. "I don't feel comfortable doing this," I said. But she already had me pinned to the mattress.

I rolled her over and got on top. To keep myself from coming too fast I thought of the movie *Apocalypse Now*, Marlon Brando sitting in the dark sponging water over his bald head, reading his poetry.

Mr. Triste stood in the doorway, red in the face. Becky pushed me off and stood up.

I saw in the movie the native's machete fall and chop the sacred cow's head off. And I thought, God, was I stupid for letting my desires mess everything up. I felt embarrassed and ashamed for taking advantage.

Mr. Triste went upstairs.

Feeling a little dizzy, I stood and watched Becky put on her robe.

"Jesus," she said, "fuck! We had our asses to the door. He saw it all."

She rushed out of the room and I heard her go upstairs.

"I want him out," Mr. Triste said. "That son-of-a-bitch."

"It's my fault," she said.

I felt like going upstairs and apologizing, but what good was it to say that I was sorry? There was nothing left to do but pack and get out of the house.

Becky returned, saw me packing, sat on the bed and didn't say a word.

"Drive me to the airport," I said. "I'm catching the next flight out."

"I'm sorry," she said.

"Bad luck," I said. "Maybe if I talk to him."

"Apologies aren't going to change how he feels. We've betrayed him," she said.

"Let me talk to him," I said.

"You've got to go back to Tucson."

"I'm sorry." This was the last thing I said to her, then she drove me to the airport and I flew back to the desert.

THEREFORE:

I. I did everything I could to save the relationship after Becky returned.

II. There was no sense in us staying together, pretending nothing had ever gone wrong.

III. Becky suggested we separate for a while to see if things worked out.

IV. We divided the stuff we had bought together: a light blue, reclinable reading chair, a drafting lamp, the collected poetry of Dylan Thomas, the complete works of Shakespeare and the Steely Dan albums.

V. I told her to keep everything, including some of the paintings and sketches I had worked on.

VI. I returned to L.A. to deal with old ghosts and to prove to everyone I knew what I was doing.

Headshots

PAYNE'S instructions sounded simple enough. I placed the yellowish, diamond-shaped piece of paper in my mouth and chewed on it, just like gum. "Just like gum," that's what Payne kept saying while we sat in the parked car. He repeated it to Cuervo, who looked at his own reflection on Payne's sunglasses, smiled and began to chew, then repeated it to Mason. But Mason declined, having once tried pot way back in high school—it induced guilt and paranoia—he did not want to chance it with acid.

"C'mon, Mace," Payne said, "I bought four hits. One is yours."

Again Mason refused.

"Very well," Payne continued. "I'll just have to save it for another time, another place." Carefully, he folded the extra hit in the wax paper and put it in his hand-tooled, leather wallet, a Christmas gift from his adoptive parents who lived in Pennsylvania.

"When does it start to take effect?" Cuervo wanted to know, anxious to get to the French Quarter.

"Give it twenty to thirty minutes," Payne said and, after combing his red hair, scratched his beard with his thin, long fingers. "You'll know when it happens. All you do then is spit out the paper."

"What happens when *it* happens?" Mason said. He looked at the rearview mirror.

"Hey, hey," Payne said to him, "don't ask. Haven't you ever heard of firsthand experience?"

"Leave him alone," I said. Mason was my roommate, had been so since our freshman year, and because he was small and extremely thin, I often couldn't help but feel brotherly toward him. We were all seniors at LSU and had come down to New Orleans just to break the routine. "Besides," I said, "it's a good idea one of us doesn't drop this shit, you know. Mason'll keep us straight, right Mace?"

"Yeah," said Cuervo, his jaw working fast. "For all we know we might start freaking out or something and—"

"Nobody's going to freak," Payne said. Of the group, he knew the most about drugs. His was a sort of socio-anthropological-hip interest. From pot to peyote. He often mentioned Castañeda's book, *The Teaching's of Don Juan* as a source of reference.

Mason spoke up, "It's getting too fucking hot inside this car." He rolled up his window, removed his keys from the ignition, and opened the door. Payne followed him out.

Cuervo, who was from Grass Valley, California, smiled at me and said, "Shit, and to think that the closest I've ever been to doing drugs was this one time I lit up my ex-girlfriend's pubic hairs and inhaled the smoke."

I got out of the car, wondering if the stuff had already reached my bloodstream and was on its way up. If acid was anything like alcohol, which it wasn't, then any sudden movements might trigger the first effects.

As we started to walk up Chartres Street where Mason parked the Toyota, and passed the mortuary at the corner, I thought about dying, but I snapped out of it when Cuervo finished telling Mason about burning his ex-girlfriend's pubic hair this one time he took her camping. "Christ, it was so dark inside the tent. I found my handy Bic lighter, flicked it, and swoosh!"

"What did you need light for?" said Mason, who deserved credit for having come up with a nickname like Cuervo. Cuervo's real name was Alex, and he had a reputation for providing tequila chasers during progressive beer parties at the dorms.

Payne laughed, perhaps because he was as familiar with Mason's way of reasoning as I was. Sometimes, late at night, Payne came to our room, wired out on God-only-knew-what, to write his anthropology papers on Mason's computer.

"Have you ever tried to put on a condom in the dark?" Cuervo asked Mason.

Payne said he always carried his on him, just like his American Express Card. "Never know when I'll be called on to hide the salami," he said and smiled.

At that exact moment I shuddered. It felt as if somebody had taken an ice cube and run it along my spine, but I didn't mention it. I just kept on walking, hands in my Levis, down Elysian Fields.

We were heading in the general direction of the French Market, which at this time of the afternoon was supposed to be packed with tourists. We had no particular place in mind; the more aimless, the better. That's what Cuervo had said.

The mud and trash smell of the river hung in the air as we walked. Because of the heat and the rain, the humidity level was high. Overcast sky meant more rain in the evening. We weren't planning to stay overnight. Mason had to return to Baton Rouge to write a computer program.

Cutting across a huge, empty parking lot that had all kinds of weeds growing between cracks and potholes, it hit me again. This time it lasted longer, a fleeting sensation of instability and light-headedness accompanied the chill. "I felt something," I said to Payne, who was walking with

Mason and Cuervo ahead of me.

"Touch the tip of your nose," Payne said and stopped. "Is it clammy?"

I touched my nose but didn't feel anything.

"My mouth is dry," Cuervo said, running his tongue over his bloodless lips.

"It's taking effect a lot sooner than I thought. Give it five more minutes," Payne said, and once again started to walk.

I heard Mason ask him if he felt anything, to which Payne said that a reaction for a veteran took a lot longer.

A beat-up Ford pickup parked in front of a rundown oyster warehouse. The black man behind the wheel saluted us. We saluted him back. Oysters, what a way to make a living!

Cuervo and Mason started humming the *Peter Gun* theme. Compared to Cuervo, Mason looked like a crawfish next to a lobster—he was that small. But under his I LOVE N.Y. T-shirt, there was a strong body. Mason had been on the swim team and ran cross-country in high school.

I knew everybody's reasons for coming. Mason wanted to buy his sister, who was having a baby, a gift. Payne came so that he could browse through all the record stores for replacement albums that were stolen from the university's radio station where he DJed part-time. He wanted to be promoted to music director before graduation.

Cuervo had all the reasons in the world for wanting to be there. All week he quarreled with his fiancee over the phone, until Thursday night when she called at the dorms and told him the ring was in the mail. Since then he had been staying up late and drinking up a storm. In the morning he managed to survive the hangovers after taking four Tylenols.

New Orleans, I figured, seemed like the best place for

somebody like Cuervo to visit and forget about things for a while. It wasn't the first time the four of us had driven down from Baton Rouge. What I liked most about the Quarter was that everywhere you stood and looked there was fast-paced action and bumper-to-bumper fun. I remembered the first time I drove down with Mason. On Bourbon Street we saw this guy go into a strip joint and just as fast as he walked in, a bouncer threw him out for shouting an ugly remark at one of the female impersonators.

This time, Payne convinced me into coming down. He knew that if I didn't, Mason might change his mind and then they would have been without a ride down.

"Wait a minute!" Mason said, "Jesus, I just thought of something."

"What?" Cuervo said, squinting.

"Xavier, my God, my God!" Mason said to me. "Man, what have you done? What if they test you for this shit before a game or something?"

"It's too late now," Payne said. "He can't throw up the stuff, he can't drink anything for it, can't have his stomach flushed. Nothing, once it gets in the system—"

"Fucking A," Cuervo said, then softly, "fine thing we've done here."

"And it's going to last for roughly eight hours," said Payne, continuing to walk.

Mason got my attention. I knew our goalkeeper had been tested for steroids. If they tested me and found a trace of acid, they would take away my scholarship and kick me out of the soccer team which meant my chances of ever making it into the pros were shot. Playing soccer was one of the few things I did right.

"I can always dig for bones, right Payne?" I said.

"You make anthropology sound like dog's work," Cuervo said.

The French Market, when we got there, wasn't as crowded as I expected. Sure, there were tourists, mostly people trying to work up an appetite by walking around the fruit and jewelry stands. Behind us rose the sound of hooves clicking against the asphalt—horse drawn carriages, one of the very few traditions, along with the architecture, left in that city.

Cuervo slowed down and pointed to a blond woman who was wearing a very small tank top rolled up in a strange way to look like a bra. She was with this older man who was trying on a pair of space-age sunglasses.

"Probably somebody he called up," Payne said. "Who would want to fuck that old geezer?"

"An escort," Mason said.

"Keep it down, guys," I said.

It looked like Payne was right though. A lot of businessmen came to New Orleans for conventions and ended up being escorted by beautiful women.

We approached the stand for a better look at the blond. She flirted with the Oriental salesman. What did she want, I thought, a bargain? Cuervo tried on a couple of pairs of shades. One of them looked like the round kind John Lennon wore, except these were mirrored.

Finally, to the salesman's dismay, the man and the blond walked away empty-handed. So the salesman turned to us and asked if we needed help.

"How much for these?" Cuervo asked, taking off the shades.

"Three dollars," said the salesman.

"Give him two bucks," Payne said.

The salesman nodded and smiled. A large, gold medallion hung from his neck. "Cheap already," he said. "Can't sell cheaper."

Cuervo returned the shades to their place on the plastic display and we moved on.

As I walked, I realized that the people going by were glowing. This took me by surprise. It wasn't so much that they were glowing, but that a brilliant prism, or aura, moved with them. A flourescense. I looked at my hands, but what I saw on the other people was not happening to me. Instead, my fingers trembled. I couldn't stop them, so I stuck my hands deep inside my pockets. Then the shakes started to happen in shorter intervals.

I caught up with Payne and asked him quietly if people were likely to notice any strange behavior. "I mean," I said, "can they tell I'm under the influence?"

"No," Payne said, "just relax, man. Nobody knows, not unless you tell them."

"I'm not telling anybody," I said, "but, Jesus, I feel weird. My hands are shaking."

"Make them stop," he said. "You can, you know."

I brought my hands out of my pockets, stared at my fingers and chewed-up nails and thought about making them stop. The tiny wrinkles over my knuckles criss-crossed, making deep patterns on my flesh. The more I stared, the more intense the sight became. Coming out of my pores, the black hairs grew out of proportion. There was a rough texture to them.

"See," Payne said, "they're no longer shaking."

Cuervo walked over and asked us to look up at the sky. Payne, Cuervo and I stood by a parking meter looking up at the clouds. Mason watched too. "Wow!" Payne said. "Check it out."

The clouds formed right before our eyes. From see-through air to swirls to white plumes, they evolved.

"Ah, guys," Mason said, tapping us on the shoulder, "I think we better move along, huh? There are people going by and looking up."

"Don't you see it, Mace?" I said, still looking up at the sky.

"What I see are three loonies," he said and egged us to move on.

We were his responsibility now, I thought. My heart beat fast—I could hear it thumping, or was a horse approaching?

"I'm hungry," Payne said. "Let's stop at Frank's and get a muffaletta."

"Can we eat?" Cuervo asked.

Mason said, "I think we should stay out of public places."

"Be serious," Payne told Mason. Then to Cuervo, "We can eat and drink."

So now we were on our way to Frank's. At the next corner we spotted a young woman trying to break inside a white Chrysler convertible which had its top up. The coat hanger she was using to open the door kept turning in the wrong direction. Her cheeks, I noticed, were flushed as though she had been crying. Every time she missed the tip of the lock, she pulled and yanked the wire out. Cursing, she bent its tip into a smaller hook, and stuck it back in again.

She was great looking. Short, feathered hair pushed over her ears, which earrings the size of an M&M's accentuated. Though her eyes were wet, they looked intense and lusciously green. Pissed, she removed her bracelets and put them on the hood and tried one more time.

Cuervo crossed the street and approached her, then we followed but stopped on this side of the car. He apparently said something that made her stop.

"You guys should pay me for babysitting," Mason said and walked over to rescue Cuervo from embarrassing himself.

Without asking any question as to why the girl was trying to break into the car, Cuervo proceeded to help her. Mason stood by and watched. Payne and I joined him.

"This is my boyfriend's car," she explained, "so it's not like I'm breaking in."

"What happened?" Payne asked. "I don't see the keys in the ignition?"

"No," she said, "*he*'s got the keys. I just want to open the car and wait for him inside."

Payne looked at me as if to say, Yeah, sure, and she just won the Miss America beauty pageant.

"I can help you hotwire the bastard," Cuervo said, his hands holding the wire steady.

"Whoa!" I said, fully aware that Cuervo was quite capable of doing so. "She doesn't want to take the car, right?"

"No, I want to sit in it," she said. Then, "Look, thanks for the help, but—"

"No trouble," Cuervo said, letting go of the coat hanger. Again, she took over.

All four of us stood back and watched her work. She was dressed in going-out clothes: gray, tight-fitting slacks, black pumps and a pinkish, long-sleeved shirt with the cuffs rolled up.

"So you just want to break in and sit inside," Payne said in a mocking tone.

She sighed and stopped, leaving the wire sticking out between the window and top. Her eyes watered as she leaned against the door and explained what was happening.

Her boyfriend, the asshole, brought her to the Cavalier for a couple of drinks, but then for no reason at all he ignored her and started to play machine poker with this other woman in the place. Her boyfriend was an alcoholic with a terrible habit of spoiling a good time after several drinks.

"Sounds like a real jerk," Cuervo said.

Throughout all this, I noticed Mason acting real jittery, not knowing what to do with his hands. Payne just stood there with an ugly smirk on his pale lips.

I knew that if I stared too hard, she might tell me to fuck off or something, but I couldn't stop looking at her eyes, her pupils dilated according to the way her head moved.

"Forget the car," Cuervo said, "why don't you join us? We are on our way to lunch."

I checked the time on my watch. It was sixteen past two.

"Yeah," Payne said, "it might give your boyfriend something to think about."

She looked at each of us, then grabbed her bracelets and put them on one by one. "This is not the first time it's happened," she said. "The bastard likes attention."

I sensed she was trying to make up her mind, so I told her that she'd have a good time if she came with us.

"Where are you guys from?" she asked.

"We are students at LSU," Mason said.

Payne looked at him as if Mason had said the wrong thing, then he introduced us.

"I'm May," she said, shaking hands.

Cuervo held her hand the longest. For a minute I thought he was going to put his arm around her. Her hand, when she took mine, felt as smooth as a flower. Hers were the type of hands oblivious to hardships.

"Well, May," Payne said, "gonna join us or what?"

"Sure," she said, then looking at the car, "why not? He probably won't even miss me."

Next thing I knew May was walking with us, between Payne and Cuervo. Mason and I fell back to have a good look at her ass.

On the way to Frank's our conversation sounded trivial, mostly stuff about school. She revealed a couple of interesting things about herself. One, she had been married to a rich guy in Lafayette; two, she divorced him after a year—she mentioned boredom as the reason—and; three, she worked as manager of a shoe store on Canal Street.

Having been born and raised in Jackson, Mississippi, she spoke with a heavy accent. Her voice, though, was suave, and for some reason it reminded me of shaving cream.

She was talking about her new boyfriend when we arrived at Frank's. At first glance the place looked too crowded, but Payne spoke to a waiter who took us all the way to the back. We watched him clear the table, then after he wiped it clean, we sat down and he brought us menus. I already knew what I wanted, so I didn't bother to open the menu. When the waiter returned to take our orders, I told him I didn't want anything. The last thing I needed was an upset stomach. I felt jumpy enough as it was.

"Nothing to drink?" the waiter said.

"Come on, X," Cuervo said, "at least have a beer."

I looked at Payne for approval, but he was scraping something that wasn't there off his hand. That's when I began to worry. "All right," I said, "bring me a Dixie."

"Creature of habit," Payne said.

The waiter repeated the orders, then walked away and brought us the drinks. May, too, ordered a beer. Immediately, she put her lips to the bottle, tilted her long neck back and drank. I sat staring at the way the foam rose and how the individual suds popped on the surface.

For a while nobody spoke, then Mason brought up the cultural scene in New York: poetry readings, summer park concerts, Off off-Broadway plays, and the abundance of art galleries. Not that she didn't seem interested, but May looked like she had started to wonder what she was doing there with us. You could tell by the aloof gleam in her pretty eyes.

"Ever been on a Kawasaki?" Cuervo asked May.

"I can't say that I have," May said, peeling the label off the bottle with her unpolished fingernails.

"Alex here likes fast bikes," Payne jumped in. "He races them in California."

"Quake City, U.S.A.," Cuervo said.

Mason kept an eye on all of us, for he probably expected a whole avalanche of strange actions and reactions.

I drank and while drinking my hand touched the tip of my nose which felt cold, just like a dog's. But the truth was I felt all right, more nervous about knowing what I had done than from the actual effect of the acid.

"Where are you from?" May asked, looking at me.

"Florida," I told her, "I'm from Miami."

"I stopped there once," she said, "on the way to my honeymoon in Jamaica."

The sandwiches arrived and the waiter asked if we wanted more beer. Payne ordered another round.

What happened next could not be prevented. Bits and pieces of the other conversations going on around our table became audible, too loud and clear. A whole collage of words. My lack of concentration unnerved me. " ... on the plane," the voices went, " ... stewardess spilled some coffee on this baby ... mother didn't complain ... she covered ... nothing like a fast bike ... stewardess got worried ... lean forward ... full throttle ... baby didn't cry . . . eighty miles per hour ... How come you never eat all your food, Mace? ... "

I shook my head several times to make the voices stop, but it was no use. I got scared. " ... it turned out the co-pilot came over ... nothing like speed, you know ... the man with the woman got nervous ... at night I used to take this curve in my BMW ... the baby was dead ... Jesus ... You know what, May? ... What Payne? ... they took him away from the woman ... If we're acting a little strange it's because ... No, Payne, don't tell her ... you could see the little stitch marks on the baby's stomach ... go around the curve as close to the inside as possible ... the motherfuckers stuffed the child with cocaine ... ."

"Christ!" I said and the voices stopped. Everybody looked over at me. Mason covered his face with his hands.

"What's the matter, X?" Payne asked.

"Nothing, nothing," I said, "I gotta go to the bathroom."

I stood up and hurried away from our table down this corridor to the bathroom. In front of the mirror over the sink, I looked at my face. My eyes were open real wide, like a horse's. Sweat drops ran from my hairline down my forehead and temples. Quickly, I twisted open the faucet and splashed water on my face. The surface of the sink warped and undulated and the faucet started to melt. "Shit," I said over and over.

Somebody knocked on the door. It was Mason. "Xavier, are you all right?" he said. Then, "Open the door."

I let him in and told him what was happening. He put his hands on my arms and held me steady. "Take it easy," he said, "they're just hallucinations. Nothing that you are seeing is real, okay. Just—just keep that in mind."

"I'll be fine," I said, opening my eyes. Mason's face looked like Mason's face. There was a slight resemblance to Griffin Dunne, the actor, except Mason had brown hair and a moustache.

"We're getting out of here," he said. "Payne just gave May the extra hit."

"Why'd you let him do it?"

"She insisted. She's done it before."

"Oh, shit," I said, "we need to go somewhere until this is over."

Mason led me out of the bathroom. When we got to the table, all the food was gone. It was as if we had just walked in and the whole thing was going to repeat itself.

Payne collected the money to pay for the bill. How could he do it, I thought, concentrate on minimal shit like adding up the bill? May looked at me and smiled. Her jaw was already moving, but that wasn't gum she was chewing. She put her hands on my arm and said, "We're going to have fun."

"Let's walk around," Cuervo said.

"Are you up to it, X?" Payne asked.

"Let's go to my apartment," May said and told us she lived off St. Charles in the Garden district.

Mason agreed that that would be the best thing to do—he wanted us off the streets. I pulled Payne aside and told him I didn't think I was having too good a trip.

"It happens sometimes to first timers." Payne said, looking at the money in his hands.

"I don't like what's going on."

"Okay then," Payne said, approaching the cash register, "let's go to her place."

We walked out of Frank's and headed back to the car. Being out again helped, but before we reached the car it started to rain. We had to run the rest of the way, not Cuervo though. He walked. By the time he arrived, Mason had already put a plastic bag over the seat so that the water wouldn't seep through when Cuervo sat down.

Payne tried to make a move on May. He told her about how he planned to buy a motorcycle and travel all over the country this summer. He was going to stop at the University of Arizona in Tucson and apply for graduate studies in anthropology.

Tuning out, I sat up front with Mason and watched the patterns of raindrops forming on the windshield. I saw the faces of animals, things, and places. My father's face appeared. I heard him arguing with somebody, probably my mother from whom he was divorced. My father was the president of a bank in Miami. He used to take me and my brother, who is five years younger than I, fishing in the Everglades. One time we saw this water moccasin cutting across a canal, then all of a sudden an alligator surfaced and bit the snake in two. My mother thought my father was a failure, but then she thought everybody was a failure. She wasn't too excited when I received the soccer scholarship. As far as she was concerned, college was for an education, not sports.

Again, I shook my head to stop thinking. It throbbed. When I looked at my watch and saw that only two hours had passed, I panicked. Things were bound to escalate.

∘ ∘ ∘

As much as I remembered, May's apartment looked impressive. It was an upstairs apartment with high ceilings from which chandeliers and wicker fans hung. The floor had an incredible lustre to it as though it had just been waxed and buffed. The most striking feature was this aquarium over the fireplace which reached the ceiling. In it were anemonies and clown fish, angel fish, starfish, and a lion fish which moved slowly all alone in one corner of the aquarium.

Mardi Gras porcelian and feather masks adorned the walls behind the expensive furniture. On the glass coffee table sat several *Cosmopolitan* and *Vogue* magazines, a mother-of-pearl vial, and an ashtray made of seashells and sand dollars.

"Is this your place?" Payne asked her.

"No, it's my boyfriend's," she said and excused herself to go to another room.

Alone in the fairly large living room, we tried not to look at each other. Cuervo approached the fireplace and stood in front of the aquarium looking at the fish.

"Check this out," Payne said, pointing to a black stereo system. He started to finger through the record collection. "What the fuck!" he said. "The Bee Gees. Tsk-tsk!"

"I think we should get out of here," Mason said.

"Relax man," Payne said. "Maybe if I find a Barry Manilow album I'll put it on."

"This guy," Cuervo said, "has strange taste in fish."

May returned with a porcelain box and sat on the sofa. "I've been saving this Columbian, but I might as well share it," she said, opening the box.

"Dig in," Payne said.

On the coffee table she opened two pieces of Zip rolling paper, pinched some of the pot out of the box, and made two lines on the paper. Payne helped her roll the joints. Once ready, she lit one and Payne lit the other.

"Come on, guys," she said, inhaling, "this is great stuff."

Cuervo and I moved closer to the coffee table. I thought the pot might help to slow the acid down. Mason stood by the wall, a feathery mask in his hand.

"Mason, you want some?" May said.

"Let's not waste it," Payne said.

Mason put the mask on and said, "Sure, why not? I'm not going to be a party pooper."

"Atta boy, Mace," Cuervo said and patted him on the back.

Payne handed Mason the joint and let him inhale a couple of drags before taking the joint back. Payne's greed upset me, but it really wasn't so much the greed as the fact that what he wanted was control. Always, he wanted to be the lead man.

So, we all sat around the coffee table—May being the center of attention—and got high. I had my share of hallucinations. I saw insects crawling over May's face. I saw the feathers on the mask Mason wore turn into a black crow which fluttered around the room and picked up a tornado of dust and fashion magazine pages. I saw another bird fly over the aquarium and dive for the lion fish. The multicolored fish blended like paint on a canvas.

After tuning into a jazz and blues station on the radio, Payne took the liberty to roll up a couple more joints, one of which Mason smoked all to himself stretched out on the couch, his free hand resting on May's hair.

May sat still, smiling foolishly like the rest of us, the absent-minded way people smile when they get high. The more I looked at her, the more in love I fell. But, I thought, I would not bother to make a move when Payne and Cuervo were trying so hard. They were flanking her.

She was saying something about the guy she was married to. Remembering how she lived with maids, had fancy cars, a house big enough for people to sleep over when they partied. She began to cry. Neither Payne nor Cuervo reacted, but I moved closer to her and hugged her. She hugged me back hard, her warm breath hitting the side of my neck.

"You know," she said, "you grow up and the older you get the more you realize that fucked up people don't change."

I told her I knew what she was talking about. My own parents were as fucked up as people can get, and neither one made the effort to change, to improve their lives. I remembered the night my father left the house for good. Very little was said between him and my mother. They just looked at each other and I knew by the glow in their eyes that they hated one another, not because of what they had become, but because of what each had depleted in the other. I tried to spare my little brother the sight of my father ranting about the house, kicking and throwing things, but he saw—he knew what was happening.

When she kissed me, she did it quickly so that nobody

saw. Payne and Cuervo were talking about the aquarium. They were tripping. Mason had fallen asleep on the couch. I took advantage and slipped my hand inside her shirt. Her nipples got hard.

She was unzipping my fly when we heard somebody trying to unlock the door. She didn't try to move away, so I pushed her away and stood up. The quick motion gave me a headrush.

The door opened and May's boyfriend walked in. He was tall and robust, but having had too much to drink, he was clumsy. His first words were: "You fucking bitch!"

"These are my friends," May said.

"I don't give a fuck who they are," he said and threw the keys at her. The keys landed on the coffee table but the glass didn't break. The noise startled Mason who sprung from the sofa and stood up.

"I'm moving out," May told him, starting to roll another joint.

Payne and Cuervo moved to the door as soon as May's boyfriend got out of the way.

"Moving out," he said. "You are moving out, eh?"

"You're drunk so shut up," she said.

Mason headed for the door.

"Ah, come on pals," May's boyfriend said, "not leaving so soon, are you?"

"Look," I told him, "I think you've had a lot to drink."

"Oh yeah," he said, "you believe—no, you think. You think I've had too much to drink."

"Let's get out of here," Payne said.

"What's the rush," the man said, "don't you guys want to stay. Maybe she'll let one of you bang her."

"Fuck you!" May said as calmly as possible without destroying all the work she was putting into rolling the joint.

"There's no need to talk to her like that," Mason said.

"Perhaps it is you whom Lady Death here wants," he said to Mason.

"Come on, guys," Mason said, "let's get out."

The man stopped him by the door. He held Mason's arm in a tight grip. Mason's flesh turned white.

"Let go," Mason said.

"Let him go, stupid," May said.

"Let's all drink and get high," he said.

That was when Mason lost his cool and let the man have it right on the jaw. We heard the snap when Mason's fist landed. Something cracked and I thought every bone in Mason's hand was broken.

The man fell against a chair. Quickly, he got up and went for Mason, but Payne and Cuervo stopped him. The man was drunk, but not drunk enough to stay pinned. He broke loose and this time attacked May. He grabbed her hair and slapped her a couple of times.

"Stop killing me, fucking bitch!" he said and slapped her again.

May got on her knees, unbuckled his pants, and unzipped his fly. I couldn't stand the sight, so I left, the guys following. As we hurried down the stairs we heard the man asking us to stay.

We were speechless. We climbed inside the car and took off. Mason drove back to the Market where nearby he found a parking space, parked the car, and got out. I was sure his hand was hurting by the way he let it hang at his side.

"Hey, Mace," said Cuervo, "where are you going?"

Mason didn't say anything, but kept walking. We got out of the car and followed him to this river landing between Cafe du Monde and the old Dixie Brewery. We crossed the railroad tracks and went down the steps of the landing to the edge of the water. Mason sat down and leaned against piling.

The sun was setting and a light drizzle had started to fall. We sat next to Mason and looked at the murky water making ripples against the rocks. This was as good a place as any to sober up, I thought. We kept looking at each other as if one of us could offer an explanation as to what had happened, but we didn't speak. Payne closed his eyes. Cuervo took out his pocketknife and carved something on the side of the piling. Mason kept opening and closing his hand, rubbing it.

I opted for the sound of the water lapping against the rocks when the boats passed, their bullhorns echoing in the distance.

○   ○   ○

After Mason sobered up, he drove us back to Baton Rouge while the rest of us slept. It wasn't until several days later that we got together in Cuervo's dorm room and started to talk about what had happened in New Orleans. Payne discarded the whole situation as a mere bad trip. "That guy was fucked up, all right," Cuervo said. But Mason, Mason was superstitious. He said it was a bad sign, an omen of bad luck. What he thought May stood for he didn't want to say, but whatever it was was bad. Payne asked me what I thought. I told him we should forget about the whole thing, forget anything happened. "Payne's right," Cuervo added, "we were all tripping anyway." We promised ourselves never to talk about it, though I was sure that if they were asked, their versions would be as different as fall and spring.

○   ○   ○

During the last game before spring break, I injured my knee. Nothing the ten day vacation wouldn't fix. I came home and found out from my mother that my little brother was arrested for possession. He and a friend were caught with a whole rock of crack in the high school bathroom, just enough to be arrested and booked.

My father and I went to see my brother at the juvenile center. On the way my father complained that it was all my mother's fault for my brother's upbringing. "That kid's a troublemaker," my father said, both hands on the wheel. He said he didn't understand what had gone wrong. I didn't know if he was referring to his marriage or to the problem with my brother. Then he told me how much like him I was, and that he was so proud of me—he just knew that what had happened to my brother could never happen to me.

That was what got me thinking about that crazy day in New Orleans.